Snowed

by Rhoda Baxter
A Trewton Royd novella

70001760047 6

© Rhoda Baxter, 2017. All rights reserved.

The characters in this book are entirely fictional. Any resemblance to actual places, incidents or people, living or dead, is entirely coincidental.

HARINGEY LIBRARIES	
70001760047 6	
Askews & Holts	06-Dec-2021
AF	
YY	

Dedication

To my family. Always.

Want a free novella?

YOU CAN CLAIM A FREE novella by joining my reader mailing list. Details are at the end of the book. ☺

Enjoy *Snowed In*.

Rhoda

Chapter 1

Tracey woke up from her exhausted half-doze when the car stopped. The driver, Bob, turned around in his seat. "We're here, miss."

She sat up and peered through the sleet splattering on the car windows. The Trewton Arms glowed through the murk. The pub in her memory, with its mass of climbing roses and warm Yorkshire stone, looked very different to the rain-dashed building she was looking at now. Perhaps this was a bad idea.

"I'll bring the umbrella round, miss." Bob undid his seat-belt, took a deep breath as though bracing himself and dived out into the sleet. A blast of cold air rushed in before the door slammed. There was a cold snap predicted. It was always colder out here in the country than in London. Bad. Bad idea.

She pulled on her coat while she waited for Bob to find the umbrella and come round the side of the car for her. If she'd stayed in London, she would have been out... hiding by the pot plants at a party. The very thought drained her. There had been enough of that in the months leading up to the sale. She couldn't face another minute of that. Not right now. She wondered if it was an option to just spend the next two weeks sitting in this warm car. Her bladder complained. No. Maybe not then.

As soon as she stepped out, the wind smacked her around the face, throwing sleet into her eyes, despite the golfing umbrella that Bob was holding over her. He had rammed his chauffeur's hat down on his head so that the wind didn't blow it off. They ran across the rain slick gravel to the big front porch. Bob put his hand on the door to open it for her. She stopped him.

"I'll... be okay from here," she said. "Could you bring my bags to the porch? Please."

She couldn't see Bob's face clearly under the shadow of his hat, but she knew he would be puzzled. His wasn't the sort of firm that dropped their clients off in sleet-swept porches. On the other hand, his firm must not be the sort that argued with a customer either, because he merely nodded and dashed off again to get her bags.

"Are you sure I can't help you further, miss?" Bob looked at the wooden door.

"Yes, Bob. I'll be fine. Thank you, though." It would have been easier to get him to carry her bags in for her, but turning up with a driver in a suit, who carried her bags for her, would only raise eyebrows around here. Her aunt had been adamant that she'd come to the station to pick her up, but Tracey had wriggled out of it by phoning first thing to say her train was delayed and she'd call when she got nearer. She hadn't taken the train in months. Being driven by limo was the one luxury she had taken up as soon as she had the chance.

Bob nodded. "I'll see you in a couple of weeks then, miss." Another dubious glance at the door. "If you need me to come pick you up sooner, just... call me. I'll come whenever, even if I have to come myself."

"I will." She shivered. She wasn't wearing enough layers. The car had been so warm, she'd forgotten about the real world. "You have a good Christmas, Bob."

The professional mask he always wore slipped a bit. He gave her a warm smile. "You too Miss Tracey. You take some time and recharge, eh? You've been working too hard." He touched his hat, a little salute. "Merry Christmas." He ran back into the sleet and disappeared. Tracey picked up one of her bags and pushed open the door.

It was like stepping back in time. The same wooden floor, too old and pockmarked to be polished. The tables and chairs were laid out in exactly the same way. The same pictures and odd 'pub stuff' hanging on the wall. It smelled different though. Previously, she'd always been in the summer, when it smelled faintly of furniture polish and, if she was lucky, roses from the garden outside. Tonight it smelled of pine trees. She stepped further in and spotted the source of the pine smell. A huge tree took up the whole of the corner where the quiz machine used to be. Peering at it, she could see the quiz machine, hidden behind it.

Three men sat at the bar. They were older now, but she knew exactly who they were. All three turned to look at her as she walked in. Instantly, she was a child again. "Is... is Angie in?"

"One second, love." One of the men stood up, leaned against the bar and shouted. "Ange! Customer." He gave her a friendly nod. "She'll be right out." He glanced behind her and she knew he'd clocked her bags. He'd have put her down as a tourist.

Tracey pushed her hood back. "Hello Mr Penworthy."

Before he could speak again, a woman came rushing out of the door that led to the kitchen. Her aunt Angie looked a little older than Tracey remembered, but really, hadn't changed.

"Tracey, love! I've been waiting for you to call. I were getting worried." The big smile that had marked the start of all her summer holidays beamed at Tracey. Angie hugged her, wet raincoat and all. "Oh. It's good to see you again, love. Welcome back."

All at once, she was exhausted. She wanted to drop her head on her aunt's shoulder and let the tension flow out of her. This place, where memories were held. In this place, she might finally be able to relax. Maybe even sleep.

"Oh, you look done in," said Angie. Her gaze flicked to Tracey's hair, but she didn't comment. She turned to the men sitting at the bar, who were all pretending they weren't watching. "It's our Tracey," she announced. "You remember her. Used to come here for summers."

There was a murmur of 'it never is' and 'been a while' and the men turned back to their pints, apparently not bothered. Tracey smiled. The news of her return would be round the village by daybreak.

Angie led her through the bar and into the office, still talking. "How are your mum and dad?"

"They're travelling round the world at the moment," said Tracey.

Angie sniffed. "How lovely. It's alright for some." Angie poked around in a drawer and pulled out a key. "Here we go. You know the drill, love. This is the key to your room and this is the key to the main door, in case you're out late."

"I doubt I'll be going out," said Tracey.

But Angie was already off, rattling off information about the pub and where Tracey's uncle was and something about a Christmas party.

Tracey nodded, trying to find a pause in which to respond.

"I've made up your old room in the top," said Angie, coming to a halt. "You remember where it is."

"I remember," said Tracey. The comment was a reminder of how long it had been. "I'm sorry I haven't been more often Aunty Angie—"

Angie stopped and gave her another smile. "You're here now, love," she said. "That's what's important." She put a warm hand to the side of Tracey's face, just like she had done when she was child. "You really do look tired. How about you get yourself some sleep. We'll catch up proper tomorrow."

The urge to throw herself at her aunt returned. Her eyes hurt, like she was about to cry. Get a grip.

"I'll give you a hand with them bags," said Angie. She bustled Tracey through the bar again, telling the men at the bar that she'd only be a minute.

Tracey's bags weren't heavy, but they were big. There were enough clothes in there for nearly fortnight in rural Yorkshire. A big mass of woollens.

They took one each and started up the wooden steps, which were so worn over the years that they bowed in the middle.

They were a few steps up when the pub door opened again, letting in a gust of freezing air. A man entered, huddled up against the weather. He pushed his collar down from his face and removed his fogged up glasses.

It took a couple of seconds for the silence to register. The pub had gone quiet when Tracey had walked in, but the punters had gone back to chatting fairly soon. But with this man, it seemed to go on for a tiny bit too long.

He was dressed in a long dark coat that was wet from the sleet outside. Something about the neat haircut and rimless glasses hinted at someone who worked in a city. He was tall and, even to Tracey's cynical eye, very attractive. He was also clearly Asian. He rubbed the fog off his glasses, replaced them on his nose and looked around. His gaze rested on the men at the bar, all watching him. Annoyance registered on his face for a second before he seemed to gather himself inward and his expression relaxed into neutral.

"Hello," he said, pleasantly. "I'm looking for the landlady...?"

"Oh, that's me." Angie dropped the bag she was holding and bustled past Tracey. "Can I help you love?"

"My name's Vinnie Fonseka. I've rented Rose cottage."

"Yes. Of course. Come with me." Angie turned to look up towards Tracey. "Will you be able to find your way?"

"I'll be fine."

Vinnie seemed to notice her for the first time. He gave her a small nod before he followed Angie, his wet coat slapping around his legs as he walked. She realised for the first time that she had been staring at him too.

Tracey resumed her journey to her room. The room was up in the eaves, past the few rooms that Angie and Phil used. Tracey sat on the springy bed and looked around to see if there were any changes. She'd remembered the room as being a lot bigger, but seeing it with adult eyes, she realised it was small.

The single bed was under the eaves and took up one side of the room. Next to it was an alcove that led to a window that stood proud in the roof. The walls of the alcove were lined with shallow shelves full of paperbacks. The other side of the room was taken up by a white wardrobe.

It was tiny and shabby compared to her room at her parents' house, yet she knew it so much better than her parents' house.

She walked over to the window and peered out through the middle of the curtains. It was too dark to see much, but she knew that below her was the beer garden. Beyond that beyond there was a lane and then a steep field, which used to have sheep on it. If she stood to one side and peered hard, she could see the road that led up to the row of weavers cottages on the top of the hill.

There was a shriek of wind and snow buffeted against the window pane. She let the curtain drop and turned back into the room. Small it may be, but it was also warm and snug and... homely. More homely than either of her 'homes' really. Her shoulders unknotted, just a little. Homely. That was what she needed right now. Somewhere homely with lots of tea and comfy places to sit and read.

Tracey sighed and flopped back onto the bed. Not such a bad idea after all.

Chapter 2

The sleet had turned to snow and was coming down in earnest now. Vinnie could only just see the road through the swirling white in his headlights. Top of the hill. The car was just about managing to keep in second gear. He was going to have to switch to first any minute. Some hill. Thank goodness he'd remembered to throw his walking boots and waterproof into the car before he left. A red pillar box appeared by the side of the road. Right. Must be near.

"You have arrived at your destination," the satnav informed him in her clear Irish voice.

Okay then. There were two cars parked by the road. He eased in and parked just ahead of them. The landlady had said it was the last cottage in the row. Green door, she'd said, but he'd be lucky to see that in this weather.

Wishing he'd had the foresight to put his waterproof coat on, rather than just flinging it in the boot, he turned up his collar again and wrapped a scarf around his throat before venturing out. The flashlight on his phone showed him that Rose Cottage was indeed, only a few yards away.

"Idyllic getaway," he muttered to himself and he slipped and slid his way up the path. "Romantic cosy nest." What a load of crap. He found the key, opened up and practically fell in. His glasses instantly steamed up.

Cursing, he leaned on the door to shut it and felt along the wall for the light switch. The heating had clearly been put on ahead of his getting there. He felt warmth against his face. Aha. Light switch. He rubbed his glasses on his scarf and put them back on.

He was standing at the bottom of the stairs. The place smelled faintly cinnamony. He went through, flicking on lights. The living room had a couple of big sofas in it and a small table and chairs tucked in at the back. There was, as advertised, a wood burning fire, with a neat pile of logs next to it. The kitchen was miniscule. He tramped up the stairs. Bathroom. Bedroom and a cupboard with a bed in it that qualified as the second bedroom. All very tastefully decorated in pastels and flowery prints and all spotlessly clean. He leaned against the doorframe of the bedroom and stared at the tidy double bed. It looked... feminine. These places were decorated with an eye to attracting women to come and stay, right? Or idiots like him who thought they'd impress a woman by booking a 'cosy cottage in the Yorkshire Dales'.

Sadness welled up and punched a hole in the glacier of anger that had powered him up to now. He had done some stupid things in his time, but this was up in the top five. He should have cancelled the booking. He'd have got most of his money back. But no, he had to be mister hardarse and say 'well, I'm going anyway.'

On the other hand, it had to be better than going home to his parents' house - where his mother would fuss - he wasn't ready for the all-enveloping sympathy yet. And it was definitely better than being in the flat all by himself, looking at all the spaces left by the things she'd taken away.

Vinnie sighed and headed back downstairs. He should get his stuff in from the car before it froze to the inside of the boot. Stepping outside in his office shoes, he nearly landed on his backside. The first things to get out would have to be those boots.

Chapter 3

Tracey was the only one there at breakfast, so she got the full force of Angie's chatter along with her full English breakfast. She switched off after a bit and retreated into her own thoughts. She felt strange ... almost leaden after a night's sleep. She had been woken up at 4am by the absence of noise. It was silent in her room, apart from the wail from the wind. No trains rattling past, no cars, no neighbours rolling home at ungodly hours. None of the everyday noises of people living their daily lives. It had felt eerie.

She rubbed her eyes. They felt hot and dry again. When she had failed to get back to sleep, she'd turned to the stack of paperbacks and selected one at random. She'd read all of these books, her grandmother's romance novel collection, in her teens, when there was nothing else to do. They had allowed her to escape the world and be someone else. Someone willowy and elegant and worthy of being loved. Now, ten years on, Tracey was a little more cynical and the stories took a little longer to work their soothing magic, but soothe they did. Even though she knew exactly how it was going to end, she couldn't wait to get back to it. She hadn't read a book for pleasure in years. How could she have forgotten?

A silence made her aware that Angie had stopped talking. She focused, with some difficulty, on her aunt, who was standing at the end of the table.

"Um... sorry, Aunty Angie, I didn't catch that," she said. Hopefully it wasn't obvious that she hadn't been listening.

"What are your plans for the week?" said Angie. "You planning to do some shopping? If you want to go into Huddersfield or summat, I'm sure someone from the village can drop you off at the station."

She'd forgotten this. People in Trewton Royd were so informal. Farmers would give you a lift into the next town. The village bakery let you have a bun and trusted that you'd pop back with the money as soon as you'd been to the cash point. After years of London, this familiarity felt somehow intrusive. Tracey realised she was clutching her fork too tightly now, as though she was expecting Angie to grab it off her. She forced her fingers to relax.

"I was just going to spend the time relaxing," she said. "You know, have a proper break. I'll probably just hang around the village and read."

Angie nodded. "A lot of people do that. Not normally at Christmas, mind, but other times. Things been difficult at work, then?"

She wondered what to tell her. The months running up to the takeover had been stressful, but that handover hadn't fully completed until a few days ago. She wasn't sure what was going to happen now. She and her business partner, Giselle, had been retained only for six months, with an option to extend their contracts if the handover suffered any delays. Luckily, they didn't have a lot of staff to move around - she didn't think she could've coped with having to make people redundant. The only person in the company who hadn't had shares in it was Sally, who was PA to both Tracey and Giselle, and they'd been able to take Sally with them. But what happened now? There would be discussions about the future of their app and she and Giselle has no say in it. "A bit stressful, yes," she said. "We ... er ... had a lot on."

"Things are okay though? With your work?"

Tracey nearly laughed. She and Giselle had made two million pounds each from the sale. It didn't feel real though, not yet. "Yes. Fine. Just... been busy."

Her aunt nodded. "You look... well, you look awful." Tracey would have been offended if it weren't for the concern in the older woman's eyes. "And how are your ... eyes?"

Finally, the question that had been circling her aunt's mind. "They're okay. No worse. No better."

"Oh." Angie's face fell. She really believed in the healing power of modern medicine. She refused to accept that despite all the eye patches and sight tests and glasses with lenses so thick that she looked like she was one bionic eye, Tracey still had trouble focusing straight. It was as though she was hoping that some miracle would happen one day and Tracey's eyes would sort themselves out. "I'm sorry."

Tracey nodded. What else was there to say? She gave up on the enormous breakfast and put down her cutlery. "That was lovely," she said. "But I don't think I can eat all of it."

"Don't you worry love. We'll get you well fed and rested by the end of the week." Angie patted her hand before gathering up the breakfast things. "Anything else I can get you?"

"No. If you don't need me for anything, I'll probably just sit in one of the armchairs and read."

"Let me get the fire going for you, then. Give me a minute and I'll get our Phil to sort it out."

By the time Tracey had fetched her book and returned downstairs, the fire was starting to crackle.

Her uncle Phil had pushed one of the armchairs across to it for her and was plugging in a lamp. He looked up and smiled. "There you go, love. That should set you up. Our Angie will be busy this morning, so you should have some quiet."

The warmth of the gesture nearly winded her. "Thanks, Uncle Phil."

He nodded. "Just shout if you need owt else."

She watched him walk off and noted how he seemed a little stooped these days. Her aunt and uncle were both aging. They had bought this pub soon after they got married and had made it the heart of this village. And when her mother decided that Tracey was too pale and too dull and too embarrassing, Angie and Phil had taken her in and made the pub the heart of her too. The tears pressed against her eyes again. She blinked them back.

Tracey settled into the armchair, moving the cushions around until she was comfortable. For a moment, she sat, with her book unopened on her lap, staring into the flames. She hadn't been sure what she was hoping to find when she'd run away from London for Christmas. Not sympathy, but at least a break from the self-absorption and the relentless pursuit of the 'right places' and 'right things to do'. When the sale of her company had been announced, she and Giselle had suddenly become very popular. There were job offers, party invitations, requests to speak about working in Tech to girls in secondary school. All completely terrifying for someone like Tracey, who wasn't comfortable in crowds or large spaces.

There had been barely enough time to absorb the fact that they'd really sold the company, so she'd parked it. Something to worry about later.

She looked at the slim book on her lap. Secretary to the Millionaire. She'd never seen herself as secretary material. Nor as millionaire material really, so go figure. Tech wizards weren't supposed to read romance. They were supposed to read... what? Philip K Dick or Asimov? Although, she'd read those too. They were fun, but not comfort reads. Not to her anyway.

Tracey opened out her glasses, with their mismatched lenses, coaxed open the discoloured pages, and a started to read.

VINNIE SAT IN THE MIDDLE of the bed, staring at the flowery curtains. He had been sitting there, duvet drawn up to his shoulders, for twenty minutes now. Trying to muster up the energy to get out. The righteous anger that had propelled him out of Leeds and all the way out here had died down and been replaced by a vast emptiness. He had booked this holiday as a romantic week away for himself and Hayleigh. The idea had been that they went somewhere cosy and Christmassy, just the two of them. In his mind, it didn't matter where they were, so long as it was warm and picturesque and they had each other. He'd commissioned the ring, so that it was just right. The one she'd always wanted. Hayleigh claimed she loved Christmas, so the idea was to take her on a cosy pre-Christmas holiday and propose, so that she could take the ring home with her to show her family at Christmas.

His criteria had been: cottage, somewhere nice, with a wood fire and, preferably, a Wi-Fi signal. He'd found a number of places and read hundreds of Tripadvisor reviews. He'd picked this one because of the flowery curtains. Hayleigh was constantly trying to deck his flat out with things from Cath Kidston — so she would love this. Wouldn't she?

Wrong. It turned out that something Christmassy to Hayleigh didn't involve snow and cosy cottages and log fires. It certainly didn't involve 'only Yorkshire'. Christmassy to Hayleigh meant lights and parties and glamour. In New York. With a senator's son that she'd been seeing behind his back for the last two months. Vinnie sighed. He couldn't compete with that.

He drew his knees up and winced at the tendril of cold that resulted. She had called him boring and parochial. Parochial. Apparently, he was insignificant enough that she could just ditch him and move out one lunchtime without bothering to see him in person. He'd only found out when he'd called her to tell her about his 'surprise'. Well, at least one of them had been surprised. It wasn't her.

Coming here by himself had been an act of defiance on his part. He'd booked the place and he was bloody well going to enjoy it. Except it seemed a pointless gesture now. Hayleigh certainly didn't give a toss about his sitting in a cold bed that needed two people in it to keep it warm. His parents didn't even know Hayleigh had left. Vinnie groaned. Not a great situation. Then there was the matter of breakfast. He hadn't had anything for dinner the night before and now he was definitely feeling the need.

Reaching under the duvet, he pulled out his jumper, which he'd put in the bed with him so that it would be warm in the morning. He needed to find the thermostat. Then breakfast.

It turned out that the instruction booklet that had been left for him was surprisingly informative. Everything was explained, apart from the Wi-Fi, which didn't even show up on his phone. He found the router and saw the flashing red light on it. Great.

He turned the heating up and while the boiler purred to life, set about looking for food. There was tea and coffee, thank goodness, in the welcome basket. And a packet of biscuits. That wasn't going to last him very long. Right. Nothing for it. He had to go out. The pub did B&B — that woman with the emo hair and the suitcases looked like she was staying there. Maybe they could do him a bacon sandwich.

The thought of bacon spurred him into action. With a proper espresso maybe. He ran back upstairs and got dressed properly. With layers. He had hoped to get away without shaving, but he was already looking scruffy. He thought of the reaction from the pub regulars last night. If they were so surprised to see an Asian man in pub, they'd probably jump out of the windows if he turned up with a beard. He ran the water until it warmed up and shaved. Better. His stomach growled. Right. Food.

It was icy. The cold nipped at him and he picked his way down the path, avoiding patches of ice. Just outside, the car was covered in lacy white patterns. Vinnie stepped out onto the pavement, carefully shut the gate behind him, turned to face the village. And stopped.

The place was stunning. The sun was just coming up and everything was edged with frost. The road that his car had struggled up the night before wound down the hill and into the valley, where the village of Trewton Royd sat like a painting on a chocolate box. The slopes around it were patchworked by dry stone walls that separated fields and copses. A stream glittered at one end of the village. The main road was lined by shops, with the pub at the other end before the road climbed up out of the village again. There were a few houses in lanes behind the shops, but nowhere near what you'd have expected. It was as though, in this corner of Yorkshire had escaped the mass rush of house building that had happened elsewhere.

Vinnie breathed in and felt the crispness in the air that he hadn't felt in years. Beautiful. What was it Hayleigh had called this lovely little corner of the world? A shithole from the dark ages. Hah. Shows how much she knew. He started tramping down the hill, walking boots crunching the fresh ice. Every so often, he lost his footing and had to grab the stone wall next to him. If you were comparing it to New York, then maybe it wasn't up to much, but really, how much more special was this place, compared to somewhere you had to buy your way into? Hayleigh had some stupid idea that romance was all about people lavishing expensive gifts on each other and going to swish restaurants. He blamed all those rom coms she was always watching. He'd sat through a few with her. He had once asked how come the men in these films were always rich and/ or playboys, were there no films where the boring, normal guy got the girl? She'd laughed at him and called him sweet.

He should have seen it coming.

The slope eased up a bit, so that he could walk more normally again. He wondered if Hayleigh even owned a pair of walking boots. He had bought her a pair, just in case, they were in the car. He'd have to take them back. Hopefully, he'd get his money back. He was probably stuck with the ridiculously expensive ring though. He doubted jewellers had the same returns policy as Mountain Warehouse. Hayleigh didn't know what she was missing.

He blew out his breath in a cloud. His parents had tried to warn him. When he had finally taken her home to introduce her to his parents, his mother had said afterwards "she's very... sophisticated" in the same tone of voice his grandparents would have said 'Westernised'. Like it was bad thing. He had taken it to mean that they thought he wasn't capable of being with someone sophisticated. He suddenly realised that they'd meant that his tastes and hers might not match. He'd always thought he was more a man of the world than they gave him credit for... but what if they knew him better than he knew himself? Clearly, he wasn't sophisticated enough for Hayleigh.

He slipped again and had to hug the wall like a friend. Given the conditions underfoot, maybe it was just as well that he hadn't brought Hayleigh here. She would have been forced to wear the walking boots. She'd have hated that. He'd never had got her to say yes anyway! The thought brought with it a grim smile. He was such an idiot. How could he not have seen it?

It was still early and the shops weren't open yet. Vinnie stopped to read the menu of the bistro, which had a surprisingly cosmopolitan offering. As he stood there, there was a waft of cinnamon and sugar. Without thinking, he turned around and crossed the road to follow it. There was a bakery. Pat's Pantry.

The smell of cinnamon buns was stronger now he was near it. His stomach growled so loudly he thought it must echo. He pressed his face against the glass. The bakery was clearly running, he could see movement in the back, but the cafe part in the front was in darkness. Dammit. For a moment he considered banging on the glass and asking them to sell him a bun. Now. But politeness got the better of him and he reluctantly resumed the trek to the pub.

The going was easier here, where someone had gritted the pavement, so he reached the pub at a semi run. He pushed the door open and went in. There seemed to be no one about, but he could smell food now, so he leaned across the bar and knocked on the door that led off it. The woman from the night before popped her head round.

"Hello mister Fonseka," she said. "Everything all right with the cottage?"

"Actually, no, the Wi-Fi isn't working." He added quickly, before she could respond, "I was just wondering if you were doing breakfasts ... "

"Of course love, what would you like?" She peered along the bar. "There's a menu just—"

"Bacon sandwich, please. If you've got one."

"Baco-" She hesitated and Vinnie could see the thought process. He suppressed a smile and waited to see how it played out.

The landlady reached a conclusion. "You know that's pork, don't you, love?" she said, apologetically.

Nicely played. Vinnie grinned. "Yes. That's fine. I'm not vegetarian."

To her credit, she grinned back. "Wholemeal or white?"

He placed his order, was given his filter coffee — espresso was too much of an ask — and told to wait a few minutes for his sandwich. He looked around the empty pub and spotted the fire. Heat. That would be most welcome.

Even the pub was picturesque in a slightly dingy way. There were paper chains and wreaths of fake holly and a real Christmas tree that smelled of proper pine. Even though his parents weren't religious, they'd let him and his siblings have a real Christmas tree. Just because they didn't believe was no excuse to miss out on a party, so the Fonseka household celebrated Christmas, New Year, Chinese New Year, Sri Lankan New Year, Easter, Wesak, Eid, Diwali and any other national or religious holiday they felt like. His father joked that they were hedging their bets.

Smiling at the memory, Vinnie took his coffee over to the fire. As he got closer, he realised that the armchair that he was hoping to sit in was actually occupied. The girl with the big suitcases was curled up in it, reading. She had dark hair, with bold red stripes in it, cut in a severe sharp-edged bob. Today, she was wearing trendy geek chic glasses, which made her look like something that had stepped out of a manga cartoon. She was so engrossed in her book, that she didn't even notice him coming to stand by the fire. What was she reading? Vinnie leaned down a little to glance at the cover. Oh good grief.

TRACEY WAS IMMERSED in a glamorous party in Milan. After a few minutes of eye rolling at the language and tropes, she'd soon fallen into the familiar world and was now completely at home inside the story. The hero took the heroine's hand and led her out onto the balcony, where lights sparkled against the ink black night. Tracey turned the page, breathless for that first kiss.

"It never happens," a man's voice cut in.

For a second, she was suspended between the real world and the story and had some hope of ignoring him and diving back in, but she hesitated too long and she was firmly back in the real world. The fire was going nicely and one side of her was feeling a little too warm. She looked up to see who had spoken. It was the man from last night. Only without the glasses ... or the city coat.

He saw her look up and gestured towards the book. "It doesn't happen. Real millionaires hire experienced and efficient PAs who can keep the place running in an emergency. They don't hire cute but naive ingénues."

She thought of her own PA, Sally. Middle aged, competent and more than a little scary. She thought 'that's right, we don't'. Aloud, she said, "I suppose you'd know, would you?"

He seemed to shrink, as though she'd punctured him. His shoulders lowered and the annoyed frown dropped away. "No," he said. "No, I suppose I don't, really. Fair point." He shrugged off his coat. "Although, I can tell you that lawyers hire legal secretaries for their competence. Even the male ones."

He looked different without a suit. Smaller. Perhaps he was one of those men who could rock a suit, but looked less impressive out of one. He was wearing jeans and a jumper. Not, she was relieved to see, a Christmas jumper. Right now, he looked nice and normal. And ... she was staring again. She quickly looked down at her book.

"I'm sorry. I'm being very rude," he said, suddenly. "I shouldn't judge you on your holiday reading. Or any reading, for that matter. It's just been a long morning." There was a low growling noise. He put his hand on his stomach. "Sorry. Like I said, long morning. No breakfast. I've just walked here and I'm frozen." He glanced at the fire. "Would you mind if I joined you? You seem to have the warmest corner in the pub."

His gaze caught hers, just for a second, before he looked away. Tracey didn't know what to say. She never knew what to say to people at the best of times. A childhood of wearing thick glasses and being clumsy meant that she'd never had the chance to practise the niceties of socialising. Books and computers were much easier to deal with than real people.

She opted for the polite company standby. "Is that what you do, then? Lawyer?"

"Commercial contracts. Nothing glamorous." He pulled the other armchair, the less comfy one, across and sat down, his hands stretched out towards the fire. He had long fingers and neatly squared off nails. "How about you?"

"I'm a tech entrep—" She wasn't an entrepreneur anymore though, was she? The minute she sold her business, she'd become a temporary manager for her little team inside a much larger mothership. "I work for a tech company," she said.

He didn't answer. She could almost feel him thinking 'and?', so she added, "I'm a software engineer, really."

She always expected a variation of 'but you can't write code, you're a girl' when she told men that, even though it happened less frequently nowadays. This guy was a lawyer and an Asian one. He probably had fixed ideas about what women should do. To her surprise he nodded and didn't look even mildly fazed.

Tracey could feel the silence, blossoming out from the gap in the conversation. She hated that. In a minute the silence would have been there too long to disturb it ... and the conversation would die. This always happened. The awkwardness. There seemed to be nothing she could do to escape it.

She was saved by Angie bustling in. "Here you are. One bacon sandwich with ketchup." She handed the man the tray. "I popped a cinnamon bun on the side too, since you mentioned you were hungry. They're made by the local bakery. We get all our bread from there." She turned to Tracey. "Do you need anything else, Tracey love? More tea?"

"Yes please. Can I have a cinnamon bun as well, please?"

Behind Angie, the man took a big bite and gave an appreciative moan.

Angie laughed. "We often get that reaction," she said. "I bet you haven't had an honest bacon butty in ages. The fancy new bistro in the village serves breakfasts, you know." Her mouth pinched down with disdain. "Costs about fifteen quid and you still need to have a sandwich afterwards. Ridiculous."

Tracey gave up on her book. She was clearly not going to have an uninterrupted reading session now. If she wanted to savour the kiss scene, she would have to read it later.

"Will you be coming to the Christmas party, Tracey?" Angie turned to her. "We have some tickets left. It's only 25 pounds, and there's a disco after. It's much cheaper than what they're charging down the road." This was followed by a disdainful sniff. "They're charging sixty five quid for dinner down there, you know. For that price, you'd think they were serving everything gold plated."

"Down there?" She was missing some vital piece of information.

"The posh restaurant in the village."

Oh yes. That. Trewton Royd didn't take to change very well.

"So, will you come? You may as well. You'll be able to hear the disco in your room, I should think."

She got the subtext. Come to the party. Support your local pub. Even though this wasn't remotely local to her. But what was twenty five pounds, to make her aunt happy. "Yeah. Sure. I'll come."

Angie beamed. She turned to the man, who put down his sandwich and wiped a smudge of ketchup off his lip.

"What about you, Mr Fonseka?"

"Call me Vinnie," he said.

"That's a nice name," said Angie. She opened her mouth, paused, then said, "Will you be wanting tickets as well, Vinnie?"

He shrugged. "Sure."

"That'll be two tickets for you, will it love?"

He looked down at his sandwich. "Um... no. Just the one."

"Right you are, love." Angie turned to give Tracey a meaningful glance, eyebrows raised. Tracey pretended not to notice. She didn't particularly want to gossip about random strangers. But then, this was rural Yorkshire. Gossip about people they knew was pastime number one. Having strangers to gossip about... well, that was like Christmas.

She shifted position slightly so that she was facing away from Vinnie and returned to her book.

Chapter 4

Vinnie polished off the sandwich and wished he had another. Hot bacon, crusty white bread with butter, not margarine. Perfect. How long was it since he'd had something like that for breakfast? Muesli was very worthy, but nothing could beat a hot sandwich for chasing away the cold. He took a sip of coffee and eyed the cinnamon bun. He was still hungry enough to demolish that in a mouthful, but he needed to slow down before he gave himself indigestion. He stretched his legs out towards the fire. The ankles of his jeans were dark, where the snow had clung to them and melted. It was too much to hope that they'd dry by the fire like this, but at least they'd get a bit less saturated.

It was nice sitting by a real fire. The logs popped and hissed. Funny how you never thought about a fire hissing. He watched the blue and yellow flames. He knew that if he looked closely, every flame had a dark space in the centre of it. A dead thing surrounded by light and heat. A bit like his relationship. How funny. One day you're planning how you're going to ask the love of your life to marry you... and the next day you've discovered she's a selfish cow. He rolled the tension out of his shoulders. Maybe she did him a favour, bailing out when she did. It would have been so much worse if this whole thing had blown up after they'd got married.

He crossed his legs at the ankle. So now he was single. He hadn't been single for a long time. He'd have to go and meet someone again. How did you even do that now? He was getting a bit old for the company socials. That was for the fresh faced new grads who had turned up full of ambition and optimism and with money in their pockets for the first time. He was too old for that.

Internet dating, maybe? He shuddered at the thought.

A log popped on the fire and settled, giving off a rush of sparks that made him jump. He glanced up at the girl who was sitting opposite him. The sudden flare hadn't seemed to bother her at all. She was back to being engrossed in her book.

Vinnie considered her for a moment. With her manga hair and odd t-shirt, she looked like the sort of person who read comic books, not someone who read Mills and Boon. Hayleigh read a lot of romance books, some with millionaires, some with Dukes and lately, many with things like handcuffs and whips on the cover. He had assumed that she chose to read them as a form of escapism. It hadn't occurred to him that it was more a wish fulfilment thing. She had never demanded bondage in bed. He had a sudden vision of her, sitting in bed in her pyjamas and felt a wrench of sadness. No more companionable evenings. Loneliness stretched ahead of him. It hurt.

What possessed him to come to this cottage by himself? He could have just paid up and left it unused. He could have gone to the pub and drowned his sorrows. On the other hand, there weren't many people available to join him in the pub at the moment. Everyone at work was either already on their holidays or frantically dashing around doing last minute shopping. Everyone he knew locally outside of work had been Hayleigh's friend first. So if he went back to his place, he would have simply ended up sitting at home, by himself, drowning himself in red wine and cheese sandwiches.

So instead he was here. In a pub, where he knew nobody. Staying in a house meant for a cosy couple, all by himself. He had been in such a rage when he left that he hadn't thought to bring his e-reader or any books. In his bag he had champagne and chocolates, which seemed ludicrous now. No books, no internet, no DVDs. There was a telly in the cottage, but there was nothing else. What was he going to do?

He wasn't far from home, but his parents were away. Over the years, his family had come to an arrangement that they spent Christmas day however they wanted. His parents went to London, where they stayed with friends and attended an annual do there. His sister, brother and himself tended to spend Christmas with the families of their respective girlfriends. While Christmas was free and easy, all the Fonsekas converged on their parents' house on New Year's Eve. Christmas was a religious holiday that didn't concern them, but New Year felt like the start of something and his mother liked them to be together for it.

A pattering at the window made him look up. Hail. Great. The roads were icy and the idea of driving back to his empty flat looked even more unpleasant. Looked like he was stuck here for the time being.

The four days stretched ahead of him, cold and empty. Maybe it was a good chance to take that break he kept telling himself he needed. Slow down. Take the days as they came. He picked up the cinnamon bun and bit into it. His thoughts ran into a wall of cinnamon and sugar and stopped. He looked down at the bun in surprise. Delicious.

"Pardon?"

He looked up. He must have said something out loud, the manga girl was looking at him.

"This." He waved the bun at her. "This is incredible."

"Sue's famous cinnamon buns. They are good aren't they." She smiled for the first time. With the small frown gone, her face changed. She looked younger and... attractive.

He dropped his eyes and looked back at his bun. He shouldn't be looking at other women, he was... well, he wasn't taken any more. Was he? Perhaps he was feeling guilty out of habit.

"They're Sue's signature confection," she said. "Have you had a chance to try out some of her cakes yet? She runs Pat's Pantry in the village."

He'd pressed his face against the window there. It had certainly smelled amazing. "It wasn't open this morning."

"You should definitely try it," she said.

He noticed her plate was empty. She had a tiny smattering of sugar by her mouth. He indicated to it. "You have..."

She brushed the side of her mouth with a thumb. "Thanks." She smiled again. Definitely attractive. She was pale and not wearing make up. Hayleigh always wore make up. He'd seen her without it, of course, but whenever he thought of her, he always saw the fully made up version. Funny that.

The girl ... what was her name? Tracey, that was it ... turned her attention back to her book.

"Um ..."

She looked back up.

"Is there anything to do around here? The internet at the cottage is down and ..."

"It's down here too. Aunty Angie phoned up, but she was on hold for so long, she hung up again." She sighed. "Annoying, isn't it? I feel like I've lost a limb." She pulled her phone out from next to her and waved it at him. "And there's no network signal. It's so frustrating." The frown was back. She looked cranky again. "It's like I've stepped into a pocket universe that got stuck in the 1990s."

Vinnie sighed. It was. He pulled his own phone out and glanced at it without much enthusiasm. "I can't check my work email," he said. "It is irritating, but I'm sure nothing urgent will come in between now and New Year." He tried to believe it. Even if something did come up, a couple of his colleagues were around to deal with it. The firm was never left unstaffed. The other year he had drawn the short straw and had to do the Christmas shift. Hayleigh had been furious until she'd found a cheap holiday to... New York... oh. That must be how she met the Senator's son. So all that time when he'd been stuck at work, feeling bad that he wasn't with her, she'd been... He winced. No. He couldn't think about that. He needed to figure out something to do.

"Is there anywhere where I can buy some stuff. You know, books, DVDs, that sort of thing?" he asked.

Tracey pulled a face. "It's been a while since I've visited, to be honest," she said. "You'd best ask Angie. The last time I was here there was the corner shop, which had a few bits and bobs... and the craft shop sometimes has stuff like jigsaw puzzles and things. Sorry. That's not much help, is it? If you're brave enough to drive in this weather, Huddersfield's not too far."

"Don't fancy driving much. I was a little worried that my little car would even make it up the hill last night."

She gave a slow nod, her gaze focused on the fire. "What sort of things are you after? What do you normally do for fun?"

The question floored him. What DID he do for fun? He and Hayleigh watched movies and went to wine bars, but he didn't do that by himself. Hobbies. He must have had a hobby at some point. What was it?

He was still thinking about this, when Tracey said, "Actually, if you ask Angie, she might have some books kicking around. The guests sometimes leave their reading material behind when they leave."

He glanced at the pink book in her hand. "Are they all...?"

She rolled her eyes. "No. This is my private stash. You need special permission to access these." Her eyes sparkled. Was she winding him up? He couldn't be sure. She wasn't looking at him, properly. Just little glances, like she was nervous.

"I'm more of a blood and war books man, myself," he said.

Tracey shrugged. "Bit of a weird place to escape to, but takes all sorts." She went back to her pink book.

Vinnie ate the rest of his cinnamon bun. He reminded himself that he had nowhere to go, nowhere to be right now and made himself chew slowly. Why was that so hard? When had he last slowed down? He finished off the bun and licked the sugar off his fingertips. If he couldn't remember, then perhaps he really needed it.

Chapter 5

By the time the weather improved, Vinnie had flicked through the small pile of books that the pub had to offer, requested a packed lunch for the next day and told Angie he would be back at breakfast the next day to pick it up.

The small drifts of snow and ice from the night before was now crunchy with hailstones. It was still slippery. Vinnie carefully picked his way back down to the single street. There wasn't a whole lot to see. There was, as Tracey had said, a village shop, the bakery, a small shop that looked like a greengrocers, a craft shop, another odd shop that didn't seem to have any theme to what it sold and, incongruously modern in the middle of it all, the bistro. Vinnie went into each shop in turn, picking essentials like a loaf of bread, some cheese, a newspaper. The bread was still warm when the lady packed it up, so he'd picked up a couple of cheese rolls as well. He munched on one as he walked. He left the craft shop for last. He didn't really need to go in, but... it wasn't like he had anything better to do.

It was dark inside, even compared to the overcast day outside. The space was narrow and seemed to be covered entirely in fabric swatches, balls of wool and knitting accoutrements. It smelled faintly Christmassy in a way he couldn't quite identify. There didn't seem to be much of interest. Vinnie turned to go back out.

"Can I help you?" He turned back to see that a woman had materialised behind the counter. He wondered how he hadn't noticed her before. She was wearing a chunky Christmas jumper with a reindeer on it and earrings with red flashing lights on them. He wasn't good at judging ages, but he'd have guessed she was around the same age as his mum. Late fifties.

"Oh. Just browsing, thanks." He spotted a few books being held together by art deco bookends which had baubles hanging off them. Closer inspection showed that they were all about knitting, sewing and crochet... at least he hoped the books about happy hookers were about crochet.

"You don't look like a knitting man," said the woman.

He glanced over. She was looking at him like a judge on the Bake Off looks at a loaf of bread. It made him want to run away. He fought the urge to back away and stood his ground. "I'm not a knitting man, no. Do you get many of those?"

She shrugged. "Not so many round here. I used to own a shop in Henley. You got a few there. What are you looking for? Do you know?"

Vinnie gave up. He wasn't going to get out of there without buying something. "No idea," he said. "I'm staying in the cottage at the top of the hill and there isn't a lot to do..."

She held up a finger. "Just a minute. I might have just the thing for you." She ducked behind the counter. When she reappeared, she was holding a slim book of local walks. "It's a bit cold, but if you wrap up warm, I'm sure you'll be okay for some of these." She handed it to him.

He took it on autopilot and flicked through. It looked like it was a self-published pamphlet and had several walks that started in Trewton Royd itself. It was only a few pounds. He reached into his pocket for his wallet.

"You could have a look in the bargain bin," the lady suggested. "Might find something that piques your interest there."

He went over to where she indicated, more out of politeness than interest. "So how long ago were you in Henley?" he asked, over his shoulder.

"Years ago. When I was in my twenties." She laughed. "Which is longer ago than I'd like to admit."

Vinnie was about to turn away, when he spotted a sketch book. The cover of it was torn. Beside it, as though it had been arranged for him, was a box of broken charcoal sticks. They were both old and tatty and reduced to a fraction of their price. Something stirred. He'd done A level art. It had been his 'extra' subject. The thing that counterbalanced his chosen sciences. He couldn't paint, but sketching... now sketching he was good at. He hadn't done it in ages. He'd never had the time. But time was pretty much in over supply right now... He picked up the sketch book and charcoal and took it to the counter.

The woman smiled as though she'd been expecting him to choose exactly that. "You could sketch some of the views on your walks," she said.

"I can try," he said. "I haven't done any drawing in years."

He trudged up the hill that took him out of the valley that held the village. It was a long time since he'd had to walk up a hill so steep. It was still slippery underfoot, but his boots seemed to be able to get more purchase now that it was less icy. The bag containing the sketchbook and charcoal banged against his leg as he walked. How long ago had he done any drawing? When he'd first moved to Leeds, he'd taken an evening art class, hoping that sketching would help him de-stress, but then he'd met Hayleigh and suddenly his evenings had been taken up with going out or staying in. Mainly going out, if he was honest. Mainly to see her friends. He hadn't even finished the evening course.

He had come out wearing several layers to insulate him from the cold. The exertion of going up the hill was making him hot. By the time he reached the cottage, he was hot enough to have to strip off his coat the minute he got into the house.

Once he'd shucked off a couple of layers and made himself a sandwich, he was feeling better about being stuck in the cot-tage for a few days. He couldn't remember the last time he'd had a holiday like this. Hayleigh tended to favour holidays in five star hotels. Before he'd met her, he had been on many a walking weekend with his friends. Something else that he'd ne-glected since meeting Hayleigh. What else was there?

The years with Hayleigh blurred into one. When they met, he had just started at the firm in Leeds, so it must have been around four years ago. She had been fun and vivacious and ex-actly the tonic he'd needed after years of being ground down in his old job. She had been good for him, teasing him out of his shell and introducing him to her friends. They'd had some good times together. If he was being honest, he had known that something was wrong for months now. It was something in the way she looked at him. Some small change in the way she held his hand.

He'd done his best - cooked her dinner a few times, even taken her out more often. In the end, he'd come to the con-clusion that she needed him to make a firmer commitment to her. After four years, it was only reasonable to suggest they get married. So he'd booked the romantic getaway and ordered the ring. It wasn't any old ring, either. It was the ring. She had described it to him one day— the perfect ring. She'd known what ring she'd wanted before she knew the man she wanted it from.

He fetched the box from his suitcase and looked at the ring. A baguette cut emerald with four diamonds, two either side. He'd had to have it made especially. It was beautiful and eye wateringly expensive. What a waste. Putting the open box on the coffee table in front of him, he pulled the sketchpad onto his lap and started to draw.

Chapter 6

Tracey offered to help in the bar. She could clear up the glasses and take food orders. Even do drinks, if people didn't mind waiting for her to carefully set the glass under the spout, listening for the tell-tale 'clink' before pouring. She'd done the job often enough before she left to go to London that she could tell from the sound when the glass was in the right position, even if she couldn't tell by eye where the glass and tap were.

The village regulars filed in around seven and greeted her with a casual 'ey up lass' or 'you're back are ye?'. They asked her about life in London and how the business was going - she kept her answers vague - and then the conversation moved on to local gossip, grumbling about politics or discussing how there was nothing good on the telly anymore. It was as though she'd never left.

As she stacked glasses and ran the till, Tracey let the familiarity embrace her and was surprised to find she liked it. She remembered all too well the urge to get away she'd felt in her teens, but it was different now. She was here in the full knowledge that she was leaving again soon. At least here, things stayed the same. Things were certain. Which was more than she could say for things at work.

The initial idea for Nifty Gift It had come from a drunken conversation. Giselle had just split up with one of her boyfriends and Tracey didn't have a boyfriend, so they'd had two bottles of wine and a chocolate cake between them and somewhere along the line come up with a crazy idea for an app that found the perfect gift. They'd scribbled notes on bits of paper, one of which had disappeared down the back of the sofa. Tracey had found it a few days later and had a moment of utter clarity where she could see exactly how to do it. She'd designed and coded it all in evenings after uni and refined it after work while working in a data entry centre.

The tech work was hers, but the initial start-up money and the advertising ideas were all from Giselle. Tracey had refused to ask her father for help. They'd set up the company, with each of them owning 50%. Where Tracey was quiet and serious, Giselle was outgoing and keen to engage. It was Giselle who tirelessly pitched to bloggers, reviewers and opinion makers. Somehow, she'd managed to get their little app featured by a popular blogger, who brought it to the attention of a vast audience of busy professionals who didn't have time to go out hunting for the perfect gift, but still wanted to look thoughtful. The product was sound, so it had caught on. They had made a decent amount of money in a few years. Enough for them both to quit the day jobs and start working for the company in earnest. The company staff were basically the two of them, Sally, the secretary and a couple of tech girls who provided customer support. Tracey liked it there.

Then, just over a year ago, they'd been approached by a mega company, wanting to absorb them into the fold. The money was too good to refuse and they wanted Giselle and Tracey (and, on their insistence, Sally) for six months in order to manage the transition and absorption into the wider ecosystem, with the option of extending their contracts for another year, should it be needed.

Giselle had used some of the money on trips to the US to make more contacts and had just been head hunted for a nice job in California. Tracey... well, she was the tech genius. There were hundreds of those in California. She knew that come mid-January, the parent company would no longer need her. She would be out of a job. But then again, she still had the money from the sale of the company. She had invested it. She didn't need to have a job.

"Pour us another, will you lass." Frank, who ran a plumbing business, counted out his money and slid it across the bar. "Don't you worry," he said, seeing her hesitate. "I aren't driving."

Tracey focused, very carefully positioned the glass and pulled the pint for him. It was funny how satisfying it felt. Despite all the work done on her eyes, her amblyopic eye hadn't quite corrected itself. The glasses helped, as did the eye exercises, but when she was tired, or stressed, or just not concentrating, her depth perception still deserted her. It wasn't as bad as when she was a child, when she had been labelled as simply clumsy, until an optician had worked out that the wildly different prescriptions in her eyes had side effects other than intermittent headaches. Her mother, who was already horrified at the idea of even having a child, let alone an unglamourous one, had persuaded her childless sister to have Tracey over the holidays, so that she could 'do her eye stuff without people knowing'. Aunty Angie had taken one look at the frightened six year old and taken her into her arms. Those arms had been there for Tracey ever since.

When she'd first worked behind the bar as a seventeen year old, it had been intimidating, but the men and women on the other side of the bar had been so encouraging, she'd grown into it. You got to see a lot of things from behind here. It made her feel part of a club.

Within an hour, she had caught up on the gossip. Old Mr Holt had died. Harriet from the corner shop was single again. Sue from Pat's Pantry had a fancy man.

"Right posh professor type from down south," Bill confided in her.

"He's not from down south, he's from over Huddersfield way," Frank piped up. "His Dad used to be bank manager in Halifax. You remember, died in a car crash about twenty year ago."

"Oh aye? What'd he come back for? Not for her — after all this time?"

"His daughter runs the restaurant in the village," Angie bustled in with a tray of clean glasses.

"She never," said Bill.

"What's the story with the new restaurant, Aunty Angie?" Tracey took the tray and started to hang up the wine glasses, carefully, testing that they were in the holders before she let go. "How long has it been here?"

"Well." Angie wiped her hands and leaned against the bar. "It used to be the electrical repair shop, remember? They closed up with Mr Whitely retired and they sold the place on. Turned out some entrepreneur type decided that a sleepy Yorkshire village was the perfect place to put his posh new restaurant. They bought it, refitted it ..."

"Do they get much business?" It didn't seem likely that anyone from the local community would go there. Even if they wanted to, they couldn't afford it.

"There's some that come over from Leeds way," said Angie. "They've usually got a few people in, but it's never heaving."

"Good riddance," said Bill.

"But why do you say that?" said Tracey. "Surely, more people coming into the village would be better for everyone."

They all stared at her blankly. Finally, Bill said. "New folk? We don't need strangers round here."

"But you do," said Tracey. "You've got all the small businesses that sell stuff. They need customers. Not many people are going to stumble across the place by chance ..."

"We've managed until now," Bill said.

"She's right though," said Angie. "We could do with more people coming in. The pub does okay, but the B&B side of things isn't going that well. We get some regulars who've come here for their holidays for years, but it's not enough."

"Have you got a website?" said Tracey. She'd never needed to look this place up on the web, so she never had. She'd assumed that it wouldn't be on the web.

"Oh yes," said Angie. "I'll show you later."

"Hmm." She thought of Vinnie Fonseka. He was probably the sort of person who booked over the internet. Someone looking for a cosy experience. Romance. An idealised vision. An idea stirred. "When's the internet going to be fixed?"

"The man said he wasn't sure. Summat to do with the weather. It's not just here, the whole valley's out."

"If you've finished gassing," said Bill. "You could get us a packet of cheese and onion."

VINNIE FLICKED THROUGH the channels on the TV and found nothing he wanted to watch. So he turned it off and picked up the sketch book instead. He had drawn the ring. Over and over, with each drawing, the lines grew softer. In the last one, the large emerald almost glowed. He picked up the box and looked at the ring again. It was just a thing now. Just a ring. A waste of money, but still, just a ring.

He'd forgotten how drawing made him feel. He had no illusions that he was any good. His sister was the artist in the family. He merely had passing ability to sketch. His sister had once told him that her art had kept her sane when she was working out how to come out about her sexuality. The confusion, the pain, all shown to the world in her art. Her art changed, Vinnie realised. He went to every one of her exhibitions, first in Brighton, now in Bristol. With each one, he saw an aspect of his little sister that he'd never known before. He looked at his drawings again. She was right. It helped. Maybe, if he could draw Hayleigh, it could remove some on the acid that twisted inside him when he thought of her.

He set to work. He drew her as he remembered her from their first holiday together. Hayleigh, wearing one of his shirts, looking over her shoulder at him. Back then she had been soft and sexy and had made him feel invincible. As he drew he realised that she hadn't looked at him in that way for a long time now. Somehow, he had been too busy to notice. He paused and ran a fingertip over the face he'd drawn, smudging it. When had he last felt anything extraordinary? Not for years.

He sighed and checked the time. It was past ten o'clock. He must have been super absorbed in the drawing not to notice. He stood up and rolled his shoulders. They felt looser. Now that he came to think of it, he felt better. Less... coiled up. He glanced down at the sketchpad again. Hobbies. He'd forgotten how relaxing they were. Durr. Of course.

Smiling to himself, he went by the kitchen to grab a glass of water to take up. The book of walks was on the table. He swept that up too. Tomorrow, he would go for a walk.

THE NEXT MORNING, TRACEY pulled on her wellies and walked into the village. The sky squatted grey overhead. A sharp wind bit at her eyelids and nostrils. She could smell the snow in the air. It didn't count as a white Christmas unless snow fell on London, but the weather didn't know that. Tracey sniffed and marched on.

Pat's Pantry was open. The bell rang as she walked in. Marzipan and cinnamon scented warmth wrapped around her, delicious in contrast to the cold. She pushed the door shut before too much of the heat escaped. She hadn't seen the cafe decked out for Christmas before. It was lovely. There were red and white cloth decorations interspersed with gingerbread biscuits on red and white ribbons hung up as decorations. The tables each had a little pine centrepiece with red and white highlights. The cake display held a beautiful white and gold Christmas cake on the main stand and a row of little cupcakes iced in green to make little Christmas trees. Even the cinnamon rolls had been twisted into bauble shapes.

An elderly couple she recognised were sitting inside, having tea and warm tea cakes. She gave them a friendly grin. Sue, the baker was sitting behind the counter. She looked up when Tracey approached and smiled. "Tracey? Hello love. I heard you were back. How are you? What can I get you?"

Of course, everyone knew she was back. Everyone always knew everything within minutes around here. She ordered tea and sat at the table nearest the counter, so that she could chat to Sue.

"How's it going in the computer business?" said Sue.

At the other side of the cafe, the elderly couple were watching, listening. Everyone also knew she was in the 'computer business' but no one here had any idea what that meant. They probably thought she designed websites. She wondered what the words tech entrepreneur would mean to them. "It's okay," she said.

"What is that you do, exactly?" said Sue. "I know it's computers, but I don't know much more than that."

"I work for a big technology firm. I provide tech support for one of their apps." There. It was easier to say now. It only hurt a bit.

"Oh yes? What does the app do?"

"It finds the perfect gift for whoever you want to buy for. It looks up publicly available information on them and selects options based on what they like and dislike—"

"I've heard of that," said Sue. "What was it called, Nifty Gifty or something."

"Nifty Gift It."

"That's it. I read about it *Stuff* magazine." Sue beamed at her. "Well I am impressed. Who'd have thought you worked for them!"

Tracey felt light headed. "You read *Stuff* magazine?" The article in *Stuff* had been what caught the attention of their new parent company.

"There's always a copy at the doctor's surgery," said the elderly gent. "I like flicking through sometimes."

"You only look at it for the adverts with the young women in lycra," said his wife, nudging him. "Don't think I haven't noticed."

Tracey stared. Just because the pub felt the same, she'd assumed that nothing changed here. Of course it did. The world didn't stop outside London. She shook her head.

"Are you back for long?" Sue came round with her tea and a gingerbread angel. "The biscuit's on the house. It's nice to see you."

"Not really, just here for a break. You know, relax a bit." She took her tray. "Thank you."

"Well, with the internet going down until after Christmas, looks like you're going to be forced to have a quiet one," said Sue. A timer went off in the kitchen. "I'd better see to that. Call me if you need anything."

Once Sue had rushed off, the other two customers seemed to lose interest in her. Tracey pulled out her book and bit the head off the gingerbread angel. Relax. Good idea. She cracked open the book and breathed in that familiar smell of old paper. It was a new book. About a sheik this time. She dived in.

The bell rang. She looked up to see the old couple leaving, all bundled up against the cold. She returned to the story. The shop bell rang again. She looked up again. This time it was Vinnie. He pulled off his hat and unwrapped his scarf.

"Hello," he said. "Still reading about millionaires?"

She checked his expression for malice. None. "Nope. I've moved on to Sheiks." She held up the book.

"Moving up in the world," he said. The sudden warmth of the cafe had made his face glow. The hat had made his hair stick up on end, making him look like the tenth Doctor Who. Cute. The word popped into her head unexpectedly. Not handsome, but attractive. She lowered her gaze back to her book, but it seemed to bounce straight back to him. How long had it been since she'd seen anyone she'd wanted to look at?

He looked at the cake counter and his eyes seemed to light up. He pulled off his gloves and stuffed them into his pocket. He had long fingers. Like a pianist.

Sue popped in from the back. "Hello, love. What can I get you today? Did you like the bread yesterday?"

"Oh yes. I ate the cheese rolls before I got back to the house. I'm going off for a walk today," he said. "I've got sandwiches from Angie at the pub, but I'd like something sweet. What do you recommend?"

"Well..." Sue surveyed her inventory with an expert eye. "You'll need something that you can eat with your gloves on, in this weather. How about I cut you a nice fat slice of fruitcake?"

"That sounds good. Yes, please."

It was like she'd walked into an Enid Blyton book. "You sound like you're going to ask for lashings of gingerbeer next," said Tracey.

"No need. I have a flask of coffee." He looked happier today. The perma frown replaced by a ready smile. It suited him.

"Good to be prepared. So, where are you walking to?" She was just making polite conversation. Nothing more. Obviously. "I take it you didn't find anything else to fill the time, then."

"Not really. But going for a walk seems like the right thing to do, you know. I haven't been out of Leeds for ages. It'll be good to get some fresh air."

"Make sure you get back before dark though." Sue handed him his cake, carefully wrapped in paper. "There's heavy snow coming, apparently."

"I'm not going too far. Only a few miles." He pulled off his rucksack and put the cake in. "Anyway, I'll see you later. Bye Tracey."

He had shrugged his bag back on and was heading out of the door before she could respond. He had remembered her name. She hadn't expected that. She also hadn't expected the little flush of warmth in her stomach at that fact. Oh dear.

Chapter 7

Vinnie crested the hill, map in one hand, the last ginger-bread biscuit in the other. The village lay in the hollow, the lights already glowing even though it wasn't even 3pm yet. The clouds were so low, they looked like they were about to crack and spill into the valley. His nose and eyes stung with the cold, but the walking made him hot and sweaty. His breath hung in front of his face every time he breathed out. By rights he should have hated it, but he didn't. He could feel himself unfurling, his sight expanding past the walls of work, car, home until he could see further and breathe deeper than he'd done in years. He felt alive and it was wonderful. He could see the cottage not far along the road. He clambered onto a stile and sat on it. This view. The sky bounded by mountains. He'd loved this when he was on family holidays as a child, but somehow he'd moved to the city and forgotten. When was the last time he'd looked up?

He pulled what was left of his bag of biscuits, tucked a glove under his armpit and dug out the last broken biscuit from the bottom of the bag. His fingers screamed with cold. He crammed the biscuit in his mouth and pulled the glove back on. The weather didn't look good. It was probably going to snow soon. He should get back.

He slipped off the stile and onto his feet. The cottage was warm and safe. He'd get in, have a good soak, then have a cheese toastie or something for tea and watch some telly. Maybe even do a spot of sketching. Or just fall asleep. Vinnie grinned. The best thing about going walking was the coming home.

TRACEY'S PHONE BEEPED unexpectedly as a message came through. She quickly fished out her phone. There was a message from Sally which simply read '*Call me.*' It was from Saturday morning.

Tracey stared at it for a moment. Why had the message not come through before? Why had Sally not called her? She wrote back '*What's up?*'

The phone beeped and told her the message was not delivered. The one bar of signal that had suddenly appeared and made her phone buzz with messages had just as suddenly disappeared.

Tracey cursed under her breath. Whatever Sally wanted, it must have been important. And sensitive, otherwise she'd have just sent an email. Trewton was lovely, but there had never been much of a phone signal in it. The mast was quite far away and the hills blocked most of the signal. With no internet access to check email and WhatsApp, she was totally cut off from the real world. Escaping was all well and good, but it was really annoying her now.

She looked up the road. There would be some reception at the top of the hill. She looked cautiously at the sky. The clouds were low and threatening. It was dark enough that the streetlights were on. It was going to snow.

But she needed to know what Sally wanted. Tracey sighed and trudged up the hill. It took her nearly twenty minutes to get up it. Goodness, she needed to go to the gym more often. She passed the holiday cottages. According to Angie, two had been let, but only one was occupied and that was by Vinnie. She tried not to think about him. She had no business finding strange lawyers attractive. Her experiences with men never ended well anyway. But her gaze kept flitting towards the cottages. One of them had lights on. Vinnie must be home.

At the top of the hill, she left the road and walked along a farm track, keeping an eye on the phone to check it had a signal. Eventually, she got a couple of bars. She sat down on a stile and called Sally.

Sally answered. "Just a second," she said, her voice low. "Let me just get into the car." There was the sound of hurrying footsteps, then the bleep of a car being unlocked. A door shut. Then, "Tracey. I've been trying to call. I've sent you a few emails too—"

"The internet's down in the pub and there's no reception here."

"Ah. Okay. Well, I've got a bit of news. They had the central meeting today."

"That's not meant to be for another two weeks."

"I know. They changed the date. Obviously, you didn't see the changed invite. I heard them discussing it when I popped in to make sure the caterers had sorted out lunch. Something's come up. They're looking at the figures and... well, I'm not totally sure of the details. Anyway, I heard them talking about Nifty Gift It... and they reckon Jared can head it up now. They're not going to need us anymore."

Tracey sat still. Her precious app now belonged to Jared. They didn't need her anymore. Jared was good, she had to give him that, and he had taken on board an awful lot about Nifty Gift It... her contract was for transferring knowhow. She'd done that. Jared had integrated her product with the existing one and now that it was complete... she had to let it go.

"Honey, I'm sorry," said Sally.

"Uh. Well, it had to happen," said Tracey. The company had absorbed the product. The last thing they needed was the inventors hanging around getting in the way. A thought struck her. "What about you? Are they getting rid of you too?" She had hoped they would see how organised Sally was and offer to keep her.

A sigh. "I don't know."

"But you're brilliant. They'd be stupid to—"

"No they wouldn't," said Sally. "I don't really fit in here, do I? Working for you and Giselle, that was brilliant. Working here... it's not me." There was a pause.

Tracey stared at the ground and thought of sensible, dependable Sally. What would she do without her? What would Sally do? She needed to talk to Giselle. Maybe sort out some kind of leaving allowance, personally, for Sally.

"Tracey? Are you still there?"

"Yes. Yes, I'm here."

"There's something else I need to tell you. I've been offered a job. At another place. I've accepted it."

"Oh, Sally, that's wonderful." A worry lifted from her shoulders. "Where is it? When do you start?"

She listened as Sally told her. It was a good job. Sally would be great at it. With Sally and Giselle both taken care of, that only left her from the original crew. She didn't know what she wanted do, but she'd be okay. She would find something. Bound to.

"I'm really happy for you," she told Sally.

"I've got to work my notice, so you're stuck with me for a while," said Sally.

"I'll talk to Jared, I'm sure we can come to some arrangement-"

"You'll be okay, Tracey, won't you?" said Sally, her voice hitching up a little.

"Oh, don't worry about me. I'll be fine. Now that I know I'm not leaving you there, I'll just walk out and enjoy my earnings."

Sally laughed. "You earned it. You should spend some of it on something nice."

"Yeah. I can't think of anything I need though." Which was true. She wasn't interested in jewellery or travel. She already owned a small flat and didn't need a bigger one. She wanted something different, but she had no idea what that could be. A gust of wind puffed into the collar she'd loosened. She put her free hand up to clutch it closed and something soft landed on her cheek. She looked up. Snow. Big fat flakes of it. While she was talking to Sally, the grey cloud had caught up with her.

"Sally, I've got to go. It's starting to snow and I've got to get back."

"Oh. Okay. Bye Tracey. Have a good Christmas."

"Merry Christmas Sally."

She slid her phone back into her pocket and looked along the track. The snow was already getting heavier. It was as dark as night. She pulled the phone back out and turned on the flashlight app. The light cut a snowy line through the darkness. White and black. Moving. It was like she was trying to walk through the static on a TV screen. No depth. No definition. It was completely disorientating. She stuck her hand out in front of her. She knew how long her arm was, which helped, a bit. Slowly, feeling her way with her feet with each step, she walked forward into the snow.

It seemed to take ages for her to get to the road, by now the snow reached blizzard standards. It fell out of the sky in squalls, flying into her face and slithering down her neck. Having stood still for a while, the heat she'd stored up had dissipated and she was feeling the cold again.

The main road was a relief. At least she could use the stone wall to provide a little shelter from the wind. The darkness and swirling white was disorientating. Which way did she need to go? Don't panic. Mustn't panic.

She turned the phone onto maps for a minute to work out which direction she needed to go in, and turned her face to the right direction. She turned the phone back onto light, but it merely showed her a window of swirling snow. It was almost better with it off. She put it away and closed her eyes, clutching onto the wall with one hand so that there was something solid to keep her upright. Her heart hammered in her ears. Mustn't panic. She took deep breaths. Right. She was facing the right way. She had the wall to guide her. If she put her other hand out in front of her, she could feel things before she walked into them. Seeing obstacles was all very well, but it was difficult when you couldn't be sure how far away they were until they hit you. She shuffled forward, trying not to shiver too much.

The pavement was slippery and steep. She missed her footing and landed on her backside. Panic flared. Flailing around frantically, she was glad when her hand encountered the wall roughly where she'd expected it to be.

"Ow. Ow." She pulled herself upright again and, holding the wall with one hand, she set off again. Her bum smarted from landing on the ground. Her trousers were now wet and stinging where they clung to her legs. It was going to be a hell of a walk back to the pub. The road only got steeper from here.

Then she remembered the houses. She should be passing them soon. She stopped and squinted ahead. She could dimly make out a light. Still holding the wall with one hand, she went towards it.

She practically fell over the low gate. By now the night was fully dark and the wind and snow was so pervasive, it felt like there was nothing else left in the world. If she weren't so frightened, she'd have cried. She focused on getting up the path to the front door. There wasn't a porch, so she hunched up in front of the door and hammered on it, buffeted by the wind. There was no answer, so she hammered on the door again. Then crouched down a the letter box and shouted into it, "Hello. Please, let me in. It's a blizzard out here. Please. Please." The last word came out as a sob.

She was about to shout again when the door open and she stumbled in, still at half crouch. Vinnie stepped back and let her past before slamming the door shut behind her. After the darkness, the hallway seemed impossibly bright. Her glasses had steamed up. Tracey pushed the hood of her jacket back and took off her glasses. Vinnie was a blurry shape in front of her.

"Tracey?" said Vinnie.

She opened her mouth to speak and burst into tears. Relief made her knees give way. She leaned against the wall and slid to the ground. Sob after sob. She laid her head on her knees.

A hand on her shoulder. Vinnie was down on the floor beside her. "Are you okay?"

She wiped her frozen gloves across her face. "I'm sorry. It was so... got caught in the blizzard. Couldn't see where I was and—" More tears came.

"It's okay. It's okay." The hand on her shoulder squeezed gently. "You're safe now."

"I really am... sorry." She made an effort and gathered herself up. "I ... just ... I'm sorry." She looked up. He was close to her, blurry and sounding concerned. Oh. How embarrassing.

"You must be frozen," said Vinnie. He stood up and held out a hand to pull her up. "Come into the living room. The fire's lit."

She knew her way around these cottages. She used to help Angie clean them out between guests. She fumbled with her coat, her fingers clumsy with cold.

"Would you like some help?" said Vinnie.

"No. No." She tried to grip the head of the zip, but couldn't. "Actually. Yes."

It was awkward and a little humiliating having a man who was practically a stranger unzip her coat for her. She felt like a toddler. Vinnie didn't comment. He looked at the coat and said "I'll go hang this up the bathroom to drip a bit."

While he disappeared upstairs, Tracey went into the living room and stood by the fire, holding her hands out in front of it. She couldn't feel her fingertips any more. It took a few minutes for the heat to wake up her fingers and with it came the pain.

She flexed her fingers, trying to get the blood flowing. When she could, she cleaned her glasses on her jumper and put them back on.

"How do you take your tea?" Vinnie's voice came from the kitchen.

"Black. No sugar."

He turned up a few minutes later with two hot mugs and handed one to her. She reached for it and missed. Luckily, Vinnie hadn't let go of the mug, but hot tea slopped over the side. She tried again, concentrating this time, and took the mug.

Now that she could see him properly, she could see that he was in jeans and jumper. His hair stuck up a bit, as though he'd not long got out of the shower. He was shaking his hand up and down, as though it hurt. There was something comforting about him. She fought back a sudden urge to throw her arms around him and hold tight.

She wrapped her hands around the mug. "Is your hand okay?" she said.

He flexed it and shrugged.

"I'm sorry. I have... a problem judging distances. Sometimes. It's bad when I'm tired or stressed."

He gave her a long look. "How long were you out in the blizzard?" he said. He looked her up and down, as though checking for damage.

"Not that long. I went up to the top to get some mobile signal and... it turned really quickly."

He nodded. "It certainly did." He pointed to her trousers. "You must be freezing. Can I lend you something, so that you can put those in front of the fire to dry?"

She looked down at her trousers. "Lend...?" She was a good foot shorter than he was and, well, narrower.

"I've got a spare pair of walking trousers," he said. "They might fit you. You're welcome to borrow them." When she hesitated, he added, "or, you could stay in your wet jeans. That's entirely up to you." His eyes smiled, even though the rest of his face stayed serious.

Tracey smiled back. "Yes. Thank you. That would be very nice."

He ran back upstairs and got them for her. She went to the bathroom to change. Once there, she checked her face in the mirror. Her fringe was sticking to her forehead in straggly ropes. Her face was blotchy red and white and her nose was running. Nice. She cleaned her face up as best she could.

It was a relief to take her wet jeans off and dry her legs. She pulled on the dry trousers. They were too big and slid to her settle on her hips. She rolled them down a couple of times at the waist to stop her tripping over them. At least they stayed up, even if it was in a hip hugging way. She pulled her jumper, which was dry thanks to her jacket, down a bit for more coverage and headed downstairs.

Chapter 8

Vinnie was in the kitchen. "I'm making cheese on toast, want some?" he called.

She hadn't thought she was hungry, but the smell of toast was too good to miss. "Yes, please."

He was putting toast on the grill. He looked over when she entered the kitchen and his expression froze for a second, eyes wide. He turned back to his work. "The trousers okay?"

"Yes. Thank you. I've put my jeans in front of the fire." She went over to the kitchen window and peered out at the white madness outside. "I'll go as soon as this stops."

She pulled her phone out. A meagre one bar of signal flickered in and out. She typed a quick text to tell her aunt that she was okay and hit send. Hopefully, it would connect when it picked up the signal.

The smell of melting cheese reached her. She turned.

Vinnie was watching the grill intently. She went to stand next to him. He tensed visibly. She moved away. "I'm sorry to impose on you."

He glanced at her sideways. "It's not a problem. It's not like you had a choice." He leaned forward and flicked the grill off. "Could you grab me some plates, please?"

They carried the plates through to the living room and sat at opposite ends of the sofa. The place wasn't big enough for more furniture. Besides, it had been furnished for a couple.

Tracey was suddenly ravenous. Hot cheese on toast, she realised, was exactly what she needed.

"How're you feeling?" said Vinnie, when she'd finished her food and sat back with her feet tucked underneath her to drink her tea.

"I'm fine. All defrosted now. Thank you so much for being so kind."

"My pleasure. I hadn't anything planned for this evening, so rescuing damsels in distress is as good entertainment as any."

"I wouldn't call it rescuing..."

"No. I guess you rescued yourself. I just provided the port in the storm." He grinned at her, picked up the plates and disappeared into the kitchen.

Tracey let out a long breath and felt some of the tension leave her. As she settled back, she noticed a sketchbook, tucked into the side of the sofa. Pulling it out, she flicked through it. The first picture was of a ring. A beautiful thing, drawn set in a box. She stared at the picture. It wasn't bad. She turned to the next page. The ring again, this time drawn with more confidence. The lines were cleaner, the shading more subtle. The next one was softer still. She half expected the next one to be of the ring too, but it wasn't. It was an outline sketch of a woman, standing with her back to the observer, looking over her shoulder. Her face was smudged. There was a strange intimacy to the picture, even without the detail. She wondered who it was. Was it the woman to whom the ring belonged?

She jumped when Vinnie returned, suddenly feeling as though she'd been snooping. He didn't comment and sat back down.

"Is this your drawing?" she said. "It's very good."

"I'm out of practice," he said. "I used to be good at faces. Can't do them anymore"

She glanced at the picture of the woman. There were no details to the face, just a hint of eyes, nose, mouth.

"She's called Hayleigh," Vinnie said. He reached across and took the sketch book off her. "She was supposed to be coming here this weekend, with me." He looked down at the picture. "But she decided she didn't want to come after all."

He was staring at the picture, with such sadness that Tracey felt her own eyes prickle in sympathy. "The ring, in the picture. Was that meant for her?"

He nodded, still looking at the woman outlined on the paper. "Yeah. She knew exactly what ring she wanted. She told me about it once. She'd seen it in a jewellers window years ago and totally fallen in love with it. It was way out of her price range back then, but she said when she came to choose an engagement ring, she'd choose that one. So... I had it made." He put his hand in his pocket and pulled out a small box. "I picked it up last week." He flipped it open. Tracey could just about make out the ring inside. "She left me three days after."

She didn't know what to say. Part of her wondered what kind of woman knew what her engagement ring would look like before she knew what her fiance would look like. Part of her melted with sympathy for Vinnie. "I'm sorry."

He shrugged, snapped the box shut and put it back in his pocket. "Shit happens. She... said I was too dull. That I took her for granted and I didn't appreciate her. That was pretty bad, but that wasn't the worst part. The worst part was just as she got to the door, she said 'I'm going to New York for a few days. I've met someone who treats me better than you ever could.' Just like that. Like it was somehow my fault she was cheating on me. Until then, I'd been all pathetic and worried. I was about to beg her to reconsider. Tell her I'd booked this place. That I'd got her the perfect ring. All that... and she says that."

"Bitch."

He didn't seem to hear. "That made me angry, you know. If she was so unhappy, she could have said something. She didn't have to go see some other guy behind my back. The next day, I went to work and... got through the day somehow... and thought fuck it. I'll go anyway. So... " He carefully closed the sketchbook. "Here I am. Quite pathetic now I say it out loud."

Tracey leaned across and put a hand on his arm. "That's terrible. Mind you, it sounds like you had a lucky escape from her."

He looked at her hand. She removed it, feeling awkward.

"Nah," he said. "I'm glad I came. This place ... " He made a gesture that encompassed the house. "This place and the dreadful internet connection and pathetic phone signal... it meant that I had to slow down. I've been forced to relax." He smiled, properly. "It's been really good for me. I'm actually feeling a lot better than I have done in a long time."

"Oh, I'm glad," she said. "Trewton tends to have that effect on people."

"It's such a weird place. It's like it's stuck in the set of Last of the Summer Wine."

"That's in Lancashire," she said. "But I know what you mean. It's the whole 1950s vibe."

"Yeah. Even the shops. I mean the village shop and the bakery is fairly standard, but the craft shop. I half expected it to have disappeared by the morning."

Tracey giggled. "I know exactly what you mean. It does feel like of those shops. The lady who runs it, Minnie, she's totally bonkers. Wouldn't surprise me if she was some sort of modern witch."

He nodded. "Me either." He put the sketch book on the table beside him. "What about you? How come you're in sleepy Trewton Royd? You don't look the type... if you don't mind me saying."

"Angie's my aunt. I needed a break from... work. I used to spend all my summers here. It's home from home, really. And you're right. It's not what I would have chosen, but it's exactly what I needed." She frowned. "What do you mean, I don't seem the type? What type do I look like?"

He held up his hands, as though in surrender. "I didn't mean to offend you."

"I'm not offended. Just curious." She leaned forward. "What type do I look like?"

"You seemed... the sort of person who would play computer games?" He looked down, a little sheepish. "Sorry. That sounds terribly judgemental. I thought you seemed like the sort of person who was more comfortable indoors than out."

"Huh." She was, really, more comfortable indoors than out. But then again... "Well, you don't look like an outdoorsy person either," she pointed out.

"I'm not. Or rather, I'm not now." He got out of his seat and leaned over the fire to put another log on. "I used to hike and stuff when I did Duke of Edinburgh... while I was still at school. I even did a bit of walking when I was at uni. I stopped once I had a job." He shrugged, looking into the fire. "It's one of those things, I guess."

"And the drawing?"

"That stopped when I was at uni too..." He put his head to one side. "Actually, no. I took a couple of evening classes when I was first at work. But then I met Hayleigh and... life got in the way." He puffed out his cheeks. "Wow. I really did let my relationship define me." He flopped back into the sofa. "Enough about me. Tell me about you. What DO you do when you're not hanging out in pubs in rural Yorkshire?"

"I'm a software engineer. I make... made... apps."

"Anything I'd have heard of?"

"Nifty Gift It?"

"I've heard of that. Never tried it though. Sounds like it could be useful. What did you do with it? Did you write it?"

She nodded. He looked impressed. It was satisfying to see, especially in someone who had no real idea what it was. The trouble with being the tech genius was that everyone you met knew it. They were either trying to take you down... or happy to bolster your ego. No one ever said what they meant, did they?

"Do you like it? What you do, I mean?"

No one had asked her that. Not in the longest time. She'd started work on the app because it was unthinkable not to. The idea nagged away until she had to either get to it or go mad. Once she'd started, she couldn't stop. Refining, testing, more refining. Trying out ideas that Giselle sourced from the customers. It all kept her busy. Did she like it? Oh, she did. Code was her language. When it worked it was... fantastic. Progasmic.

Now, she spent time teaching other people how to mess with her product. Jared's guys were good. The best. He had hinted that they could use someone like her. Not working on

Nifty Gift It — she was too close to that — but on some other project. It wouldn't be the same. She missed her little app. It wasn't hers anymore. She didn't think she could bear to stand around watching it belong to someone else.

She looked at Vinnie and saw him watching her, eyebrows raised. When she still didn't answer, he nodded.

"I take it the answer's no," he said.

"I like my work. It's just... different now."

"Work would be so much easier, if it didn't involve people," said Vinnie. "I think that all the time. Contracts — nice, easy things. Fun, even. But the clients..." He shook his head. "Of course, without clients there wouldn't be any contracts, so we have to grin and bear it."

"Yeah. Something like that."

The wind screamed and a window rattled. Tracey looked at the fire and thought how lucky it was that Vinnie had been renting the cottage. If it had been empty. Or he had been out... ugh. It didn't bear thinking about. It would have taken her hours to get back, slip sliding in the darkness that looked the same in all directions.

It could have all be awful, but it had turned out rather well, instead. She was warm now and comfortable. Vinnie was nice too. Easy to talk to. When was the last time she'd sat companionably on the sofa with a guy? Or with anyone. Even chats with Giselle had petered out. She missed having Giselle to talk to. Ever since the sale, things had been slowly eroding. The money was a pain too. She'd done sensible things — paid off her mortgage, cleared her other debts —she was her father's daughter. But there was still far too much of it left. It sat there, like a rock in the background whenever she met new people.

If she told them, she started wondering if they were only being friends with her because of it. If she didn't tell them, it sat in her chest, a little chittering monster of a secret. She couldn't get away from it.

"Vinnie," she said. "If you had a million pounds, what would you do?"

He looked thoughtful. "A million pounds isn't an awful not these days. I could spend that easily."

"What on?"

"Well." He stretched out his legs and settled back in his seat. "I'd pay off my mortgage, then my sister's and my brother's. That'd wipe out half of it. I'd put a decent chunk of it in a pension fund so that I could retire whenever I felt I'd had enough. That's not going to leave more than a couple of hundred thousand... I'd probably see if I can do something useful with it like give it to a charity to do a specific thing. Or maybe set up a scholarship fund for gifted kids who needed help getting an education. Or a start-up fund or something like that."

"You'd give it away? That's nice of you."

He gave a little half smile. He had, she noticed, a very nice smile. Warm. Sexy.

"My mum was brought up Buddhist and they have a saying... that some of your salary you should spend, some of it you should save and some of it you should give away... or something to that effect. Funny really. All that stuff you never really considered when you were growing up. It sort of seeps in somehow."

"You're Buddhist then?"

"Me? Oh no. Mum and Dad — she was brought up Buddhist, he was brought up Catholic. Neither of them particularly believed, so they decided we could choose when we grew up. We all chose not to. Although my sister had a brief flirtation with shamanism. That wasn't so much about religion as dope, I think." His smiled widened when he mentioned his siblings. "She was a bit wild, my sister. I think she was trying to figure out who she was. She's settled down a lot since."

"Sounds like you're close." She had no siblings or cousins. Coupled with her own social awkwardness, it made for a lonely childhood. Being the clumsy kid with the bulbous glasses meant that she didn't have many friends at boarding school. Her parents were well off, but not influential enough to get her any cache with any of the school cliques. Here, in the village, people had placed her: Angie's niece, the lass from the pub. It was more neutral. She wasn't close enough to anyone for them to judge her and they accepted because they liked Angie. It was probably why she loved it so. They made room for her and their community joined up seamlessly around her. "Must be nice having brothers and sisters."

Vinnie shrugged. "I suppose," he said. "We annoy the hell out of each other if we're together for more than a few days, but I guess, deep down, we're pretty fond of each other." Another smile.

The wind beat against the window again. Vinnie went over and looked out. "It's still coming down," he said. "It's a good eight inches already."

She joined him at the window, peering out. If she pressed her face against the cold glass, she could make out the light from the streetlamp. Just. More telling was the layer of white that had collected on the sill. Vinnie was right. It was already several inches deep. She drew back and was suddenly aware of how close he was.

He was still leaning into the window, his hands cupped around his temples so that he could see out. He was close enough to touch. It wouldn't have been an issue, if it wasn't for the fact that she suddenly wanted to touch him. She wasn't entirely sure why. Just because he was warm and human and standing there? Or was there more?

"If it carries on like this," he said, still looking out. "You'll have to stay here tonight. I can sleep on the sofa." He pulled back and turned. "You can have the bed."

Up close, she could see how long his eyelashes were. And the deep molten brown of his eyes. He was, she had to face it, attractive. She took a step backwards, away. Very attractive. But still pretty much a stranger. And she knew that she and attractive men were never a great combination. They made her nervous and being nervous made her clumsy.

"I'll take the sofa," she said. "You shouldn't be turfed out of your bed just because I was stupid enough to get caught in the bad weather."

"It's a freak snow storm, not regular bad weather and I don't mind, honestly." He gave her that half smile again. "It's nice to have company, to be honest. Stops me brooding."

"Right. Well, if I need to stay here, I will take the sofa. I'm smaller. I'll be more comfortable. Your long legs won't fit on here." Drat. Why did she have to mention legs? Now she wanted to check out how long his legs were. And she'd just drawn attention to how short her own were. Bugger.

Vinnie seemed to be grappling with some sort of internal dilemma. "Okay," he said finally. "Fine. You have the sofa. There's lots of spare blankets and lots of cushions and things."

"It'll stop snowing soon anyway and I'll be off."

"Yes. Good." He stood by the side of the sofa for a minute, awkwardness stretched between them. "Um... shall we see what's on telly?"

"Yes. Let's." Something else to focus on. Good idea. She watched as he sat down again and pointed the remote control at the telly. He was a nice man, she decided. She'd met nice men before. She'd never been particularly attracted to one... not before.

She sighed. She was getting weird and man obsessed now. That's what happened when she had nothing to focus on. Her mind went off and noticed unsuitable things about how attractive blokes were. Even if they were, strictly speaking, blokes she didn't know well enough to be attracted to. She didn't know anything about flirting, so she tended to go weird on them until they lost interest. Or worse, they kept buying her drinks until there were fumbling kisses, booze fuelled sex and awkward exits in the morning.

She glanced at Vinnie. He probably wouldn't fall into the 'take advantage of the weird girl' camp. Which meant she'd have to stay away from him. Great. She'd have a crush on this poor man now, until she got over it. All she could do was hope he didn't notice.

He flicked through the channels until it came to *Midsomer Murders*. "I like this program," he said, half apologetically. "I haven't watched it in ages. Do you mind?"

"Not at all. I think I might have seen this one already..." She knew who the murderer was. *Midsomer Murders* was one of the few things she watched — mainly because it was on at a time when she couldn't work any longer and needed to watch something to get her brain to stop fizzing.

"Oh." He reached for the remote control again.

She put her hand out to stop him. "Don't worry. I can't remember who did it." Her fingers grazed his arm. They both looked at it. She snatched her hand back. He pointedly looked at the telly. Awkward. Awkward, awkward.

Tracey kept her eyes on the screen and eventually sank into the story. At the next ad break, she glanced over and saw that Vinnie had fallen asleep. He looked gorgeous in repose, with his long lashes and honey toned skin. His features were sharp and well defined. It was as though he'd been drawn with a Sharpie in a world of people drawn in soft pencil.

Quietly, she padded across to the window to check on the weather. Things had calmed down somewhat, but snow still drifted down lazily. It wasn't as heavy as before, but it was still going. There was at least a foot of snow already and it would only get worse in the night. Who knows how deep it would be by morning. Staying overnight in the warm cottage, with the hot man, was tempting, but it could mean that they were snowed in. She looked over at Vinnie. He ate his breakfasts in the pub and tended to buy lunch from Pat's Pantry. She was willing to bet he had no provisions in the cottage, save a few bits of bread and cheese. If they ended up snowed in here, they would starve.

"Vinnie?"

He woke up with a start. "Wha—?" He looked around. "Oh, sorry. Fell asleep."

"Vinnie, how much food do you have in?"

He shrugged, rubbing his eyes. "A few bits and pieces. Nothing much. Why?"

"The wind's died down, but the snow is still coming. I think it might be a good idea to head down to the pub before it gets so deep that we can't get out the front door."

"What?" He came over to stand beside her and look out the window. "Oh. Right." He gave her a quick glance. "Are you sure?"

"It'll be pretty horrible getting out there tonight, but it'll probably be worse trying to wade through waist deep snow tomorrow. At least the wind's gone and we can see where we're going at the moment."

"I don't know. What if it gets worse again..."

"Either way, we can't get stuck here. There's nothing to eat."

He stared at her for a moment, frowning, then sighed. "You're right. Bugger it. I'll have to get into my manky walking things and go out again. Bugger."

"You should probably bring a change of clothes. If it gets really bad, you could be stuck in the pub for a while."

He nodded. "Give me a minute." He sighed again and disappeared upstairs.

While he was out, Tracey quickly changed back into her trousers. They were still damp, but they were warm and clammy, rather than cold and clammy. It wouldn't last long once they got outside, but small mercies and all that.

When Vinnie returned, he brought her coat with him. They zipped themselves up and pulled on hats and gloves like polar explorers. Finally, Vinnie turned out the lights and opened the front door. A packed ridge of snow about a foot high greeted them. Tracey stepped over, placing her feet as far forward as she could, to minimise the snow coming in. It didn't help. A small slide of snow ended up on the carpet. She trudged out. Her feet sank into the new snow.

All sounds were muted by the blanket of white. Her footsteps sounded unnaturally loud as she crunched her way to the road. She could hear Vinnie crunching along behind her. When she reached the road, the steepness of it took her by surprise and she ended up falling backwards, arms out, on the snow. Vinnie helped her up.

"Are you sure this is the best idea?" he said.

She nodded. "I've seen it before. This valley is like a bowl, snow just piles into it. You can be snowed in for days."

They started down the hill cautiously. It was slow going. The snow compacted underfoot, which made it easier to walk on, but the slope was so steep that they had to hold onto the wall to keep upright.

"I wish I had a toboggan," Vinnie said. "We'd get down this hill in no time."

Tracey laughed. She'd had that very thought. "Except, we wouldn't be able to stop and we'd end up in the stream."

"Yes, well, that is a risk."

She slid and lost her balance. He grabbed hold of her, helped her upright, and let go. The next time she slipped, he took her arm and tucked it into the crook of his elbow. They relaxed into each other's company, keeping each other upright as they walked. As the road evened out, they were even able to chat. Tracey told him about the harsh winters in Trewton and he told her about the classical beauty of winter in Oxfordshire.

Chapter 9

It took them ages to get to the village. The street was deserted, but there were signs that other people had walked through the snow. The prints all seemed to be going towards the pub, which glowed like a beacon in the darkness. Snow fell gently on them as they walked up the path.

Now that there were buildings to give her a bit more perspective, Tracey felt less disorientated. She didn't try to remove her hand from the crook of Vinnie's arm. He didn't seem to notice.

The door to the pub opened to a blast of warmth and noise. Tracey and Vinnie staggered in, half blinded by the sudden light. When her eyes had adjusted, Tracey realised that most of the village had congregated there.

"Tracey, love!" Angie rushed over and hugged her. "We were worried sick. We had no idea where you were." She looked up at Vinnie, then back to Tracey. Uh oh.

"I went up the hill to get some phone reception," Tracey said, quickly, before her aunt got ideas. "I got caught in the blizzard. Luckily, Vinnie was at the cottage and let me in. We... I thought it was better to try and get down here, rather than be stuck up there with nothing to eat."

"I have nothing in but biscuits," said Vinnie, cheerfully. He pulled his hat and gloves off and shook snow off them.

"Well, we've got soup and rolls at the bar." Angie smiled at them. "We've had all sorts of people coming in. Local folk, mostly, but a few people who were driving through and had to abandon their cars because it was too slippery." She ushered them in. "We're making up beds for as many as we can."

"I'll help." She'd done maid duty at the B&B often enough to know what to do. She knew better than to offer to do soup duty. In the state she was in, the task of ladling hot liquid into containers was going to be impossible.

"You get yourself some soup first, love. Then we'll see."

The bar was being manned by Harriet who worked in the corner shop. She seemed to recognise Vinnie immediately and served him a big bowl of soup. "It's Vinnie, isn't it?" she said, as she handed him a bread roll.

Vinnie smiled. "That's right."

"Funny," said Harriet, as she got a bowl off the stack. "You don't look like a Vinnie."

Was she flirting with him? Tracey felt a stab of irritation. She shot a glance at Vinnie; he was looking puzzled.

"What's a Vinnie supposed look like?" he said.

"I dunno. More ... tough, you know. Butch."

"So basically, all men called Vinnie should look like Vinnie Jones?" he said. "What if they're called Vincent? Who do they look like?"

Harriet glanced at him from under her lashes. Yep. She was definitely flirting. "Vincent Van Gogh?" She passed his soup across. "He's alright."

"Vincent Price?" Tracey cut in. This soup was taking a ridiculously long time.

Vinnie grinned at her. "I hope not!"

She felt the warmth of a joke shared. Vinnie moved along.

Harriet watched him leave until Tracey cleared her throat. "Oh hello, Tracey. Soup for you too?" said Harriet, with none of the warmth she'd shown Vinnie.

The pub got more crowded as the night wore on. A frightened looking man came in to say that he'd left his family in the car over the hill and could someone come help. A few men grabbed torches, shovels and blankets and went out. They returned an hour later with the couple and two tired and hungry children who had had to be carried all the way across. Tracey helped to settle them into one of the rooms.

Closing time came and went, but no one was going anywhere. Tracey spent most of the night running around, finding bedding and blankets. Rooms had to be shared. She was grateful that her little room up in the eaves was too small to fit another bed into it. She noticed as she passed through that Vinnie seemed to have settled into the crowd. At one point she saw him in the kitchen, washing up soup bowls. Harriet was drying up, chatting to him. Clearly, she had her eye on him. Tracey noted it, but was too busy to do anything about it. She wasn't sure what she'd do anyway.

VINNIE HAD A PULL OUT sofa in a room where two other people were already asleep on the bed. He lay there, staring at the ceiling. This was certainly not how he'd pictured this weekend going. Thank goodness Hayleigh wasn't there. She'd have had a blue fit having to slum it. On the other hand, if she hadn't thrown a spanner in the works, he would have been organised and done the food delivery as planned. He and Hayleigh would have been able to sit tight in the cosy cottage and wait for the weather to clear. None of this would have happened.

But then he wouldn't have had the surreal trek down the valley with Tracey. He thought of the look on her face when she had stumbled into the house. She had been terrified. He wasn't sure he entirely understood the problem with her sight, but to be out in a snowstorm in the dark was a pretty scary thing at the best of times. If, as she said, she couldn't judge depth and distance, it must have been a completely freaky experience. Yet she'd pulled herself together and got on with things. He could barely begin to imagine how much strength it took to do that.

He pictured the determined set of her face and smiled into the darkness. He liked Tracey. More than that, if he was honest. When they'd got into the pub, he'd been careful to give her some space, but when she stopped by to chat, his whole body prickled with awareness.

He thought back to the moment in the cottage, she'd walked into the kitchen wearing those trousers that were too big for her. The sight of her standing there, dishevelled and defying him to comment, had set off something primal in him. An urge to stride across and taste her. To feel her too pale skin slide against his. Reality had reasserted itself in an instant, but that moment of attraction had surprised him with its strength. He had only been single for three days. He couldn't do anything about his attraction to Tracey, because it was probably just his body recoiling from Hayleigh. Because he liked Tracey. Genuinely. As a person. She was more than just a body to clasp to him in the snow.

He briefly thought of Harriet. Now there was a body which was willing to be clasped. She had all but pinched his arse whilst he was doing the washing up. She was, older, attractive and... well, certainly willing. He had turned her down as tactfully as he could. He might even have been too subtle. He wasn't totally sure she'd actually got the message.

Vinnie shook his head. Yes, this was definitely not turning out how he'd expected it to. He had a crush on a girl who was too spiky to like him, whilst at the same time being propositioned by the lady who ran the corner shop. It was definitely going to be a holiday to remember.

Chapter 10

By the time she woke up the next morning, Tracey had an idea about how to help her aunt. She wanted to talk to Angie about it, but as soon as she got downstairs, she was put in charge of frying bacon. Instead of the usual full English, Angie had opted for huge mounds of bacon or egg sandwiches and tea or coffee. Harriet had brought round what was left of her stock of fresh milk, so there was cereal for the children. The pub was now the centre of operations for the town.

After breakfast, all available spades, shovels and brooms were pressed into service and groups of people were sent out to clear paths. With the phones down, Angie made lists of people who were elderly, sick or otherwise vulnerable. Tracey, Angie and Sue from the bakery made up food parcels to be taken out in case anyone was in dire need.

Standing behind the bar, wrapping parcels of food, Tracey spotted Vinnie, bundled up against the cold. He waved to her and came over.

"I didn't get a chance to thank you," he said.

"What for?"

"For making me come down here. If you hadn't showed up, I'd have sat there all smug and not even thought about the weather until I ran out of food." He looked over his shoulder. "And I'd have missed all this. I'd hate to think that all this was happening and I hadn't even thought to help." He looked back at her and smiled. "So... thank you. I owe you."

"I'll bear that in mind." She deftly wrapped another parcel. She was getting fast at doing them. Giselle would have choked on her quinoa to see her making beds and cooking. "What's Uncle Phil got you doing now?"

"I'm heading out to help clear some paths," he said.

"That's nice of you to help," said Tracey. "You're not even local."

He looked surprised. "I'd glad I can help."

She beckoned him closer. He leaned across the bar towards her. She whispered, "I think Harriet might have plans for you."

He straightened up and pulled a face. "I know. You know, she's got some space in her house. Cosy, but, in these difficult times, she'd have been willing to squeeze me in," he said with a perfectly straight face.

Tracey giggled. "Did you tell her things haven't got that desperate yet?"

"I offered to let Angie know so that any new waifs and strays could be sent to hers."

"You're a wicked man."

"Me?" He made a shocked face. "I'd better go," he said. "I'll see you later."

She waved him off. She must have remained staring after him because Angie's voice made her jump.

"He seems nice," said Angie. She had a pile of clean tea towels under her arm. She nodded to where Vinnie had disappeared. "He's mucking in too, even though he's a guest. Seems a good lad. Not too foreign."

"He's from Wantage."

"Exactly. Not like he's from Bradford."

With that comment, her aunt went back into the kitchen, leaving Tracey baffled.

VINNIE WAS BOILING. Shovelling snow was hard work, especially as there was nowhere to put it apart from piling it on top of the snow that was already on the side of the path. The group had cleared narrow paths on the pavements and checked on all the houses in that particular street now. It was strange to be standing waist deep in a trench of snow, in the middle of a normal street. He looked across at the nearest window. A small boy waved at him. He waved back.

He'd already removed his jacket and tied it around his waist. He wondered if he could do the same with his jumper. Some of the other men were down to t-shirts now. He put down his snow shovel and pulled off his jumper.

Phil, who had just knocked on the last door in the cul-de-sac came back out. "That's the lot, lads. Let's head back." He gave them all a nod in turn. "Take your time getting back, if you like. Or our Angie will have you out on errands again."

"Where are you going then, Phil?" said one of the others.

"Me? I'm going to go stand by the church wall and have a smoke," said Phil. "Don't you lot show me up."

The men ambled off, complaining that the only place they wanted to go to was the pub, but the pub was full of bossy women. Vinnie tied his jumper on top of his coat and picked up the snow shovel. He had enjoyed the work, but his hands and back were starting to feel it. He followed Phil back towards the pub. When they neared the church yard, Phil leaned against the snowy wall and lit a cigarette.

Vinnie carried on past him until he was alongside the church. He paused to look at the view. Now that the snow had stopped the air had a crystalline clarity about it. The hillside was a vision of dazzling white.

The church itself had a thick layer of snow over the roof. The gravestones stood out, dark against the white. It was just begging to be sketched. He pulled out his phone and took a couple of pictures. They would be something to work from. There was still no reception on his phone, he noticed. As he put it back in his pocket, he thought of Tracey. It was her simple question 'what do you do for fun?' that had taken him back to drawing. Meeting her had changed his holiday from one full of brooding and resentment to one of rediscovering the things that made him happy. He smiled. Tracey made him happy too.

TRACEY STOOD INSIDE the church, patiently waiting for the vicar to tell her where to put the stack of blankets she'd brought over. The idea she'd had overnight was playing over in her mind. Giselle, in her quest for 'champions' for Nifty Gift It had made a long list of contacts who were lifestyle bloggers. If Tracey could get a couple of them to visit the Trewton Arms, preferably in the summer, it would get the pub some attention. With her London adapted eye, Tracey could see that the very things that made the village feel isolated and closed to some, would make it look authentic and quaint to others. There was an appetite for all things different and off the beaten track at the moment. If they could just tap into some of that enthusiasm, they could bring some much needed tourism money into the village.

Sue's bakery deserved some recognition and there was the bistro to cater for those with more cosmopolitan tastes. The lack of phone signal was a problem, but, she was sure it could be spun as part and parcel of the experience. Summer holidays like they used to be ... or something like that. Giselle would know.

The vicar turned up and she gratefully handed over the bags she'd brought over. She asked the vicar if she could take a couple of photos inside the church. She was trying to record the way the village pulled together to make sure that the elderly and vulnerable were okay in the snow. She needed to talk to Angie and explain the plan. If she took a few photos and gave Angie some contacts, she was sure her aunt would be able to get the story put into the local newspapers. Who knows, with the level of human interest... maybe even a national paper.

Tracey had been in the national newspaper once, when Nifty Gift It was first sold. It has been a desperately difficult experience for her, but Giselle had been delighted with the coverage. This time, she reflected, she would make sure she stayed on the right side of the lens. She called her goodbye to the vicar and stepped out, still thinking about what she could do.

VINNIE CARRIED ON ALONG the path they'd cleared until he was around the corner. A figure appeared at the church door, pulling the door shut. The streak of red on black told him it was Tracey. She pulled her collar up, but didn't bother with her hood. She was frowning as though thinking deeply about something.

Vinnie smiled. If anyone needed to unbend a little and enjoy herself, it was Tracey. He crouched down so that she didn't see him and gathered up a handful of snow. This was good snowballing snow. He made a couple of snowballs and waited until she was within range before standing up and pelting her.

Tracey shrieked as the snowball landed in her hair. She looked up, shaking snow off her head. "You."

She grabbed a handful of snow and threw it back at him. She didn't quite have the range. He chucked another snowball at her. She dodged and ran forward.

Her next snowball came pretty close. He took his eyes off her to get more ammunition and suddenly, she'd cannoned into him and pushed him over. He landed in the bank of snow, flat on his back. Tracey landed on top of him. She pushed against his chest to raise herself off him and said, "you git."

She was so close. Her hands were on his chest. Her lips were only a few inches away. Suddenly, he wanted, more than anything, to see what those lips felt like. She was so delectable — he loved everything about her. Even those horrendously hipsterish glasses. His breath came short. So close. All he had to do was lift his head a bit. Just ... a ...

"You alright there?" Phil's voice came across. He couldn't see him because of the snow and Tracey blocking his view.

"Fine. Uncle Phil. Both fine." Tracey's voice cracked a little. "I'll just, get off you..." she said, her face flushing red. She wriggled backwards and tried to struggle back upright.

Sudden pain seared his groin. In trying to get up, she'd accidentally kneed him in the groin.

"Oh. Shit. I'm so sorry. I didn't mean to — Oh god. Here let me help you up. Are you okay?" She was upright now and offering him a hand.

He ignored her hand and struggled up into a sitting position. The pain receded from blinding to mere agony.

"Are you okay?" she said, fluttering slightly with an anxious expression.

"Yah," he said through his teeth.

"Bit harsh, that," said Phil. "He only threw a snowball at you."

"I didn't mean—" She stopped and looked from him to Phil and back again. Phil was grinning. Vinnie scrambled up to his feet and managed a tight smile.

"You're winding me up," she said. "I'm going back to the pub."

She set off. Phil gave Vinnie a sympathetic look and went after her. Vinnie sighed and, limping slightly, followed. A clump of snow that had caught in his hair fell off and slid down his neck. Ugh. Great.

Chapter 11

Vinnie sat at a table in the pub, feeling warm and sated after a decent meal. He had a pint, which he was drinking slowly. He didn't need a headache tomorrow. The exertion from the day was catching up with him and he was struggling to stay awake.

The pub was less crowded that evening, but still busy. Most of the people who had crashed overnight had made their way home in the brighter light of day. Around the bar, Angie, Phil, the vicar and a few other key players in the village were catching up on what was going on. Behind them, Tracey was sitting at the bar, watching the TV screen which was showing the news. Every so often she would pull out her phone, look annoyed, and put it back.

With her colourful hair and chunky glasses, she looked out of place in the cosy pub setting, but having seen her in action, bundling up food parcels and providing reassurance to frightened people that help was on its way, he knew she belonged to this community. If she hadn't done before, she certainly did now. He noticed the subtle change in the way people spoke about her. 'Young Tracey' had become 'Our Tracey' to most. She had been there when she was needed. She belonged. He wondered if Tracey herself had noticed.

He felt as though he belonged too, in a weird way. Most people seemed to know his name now. Of course, he was easy to identify as the only non-white person in the snowed in village, but still. It was as though, by helping out, he'd earned an honorary place in the village, temporarily at least. He liked that. It had been a long time since he'd felt any sense of belonging.

He smiled and took another sip of his pint. He felt... content. It was something else he hadn't felt in a long time, which was strange considering he'd been about to get engaged a few days ago. He had thought his life was perfectly well organised, but how could it have been if he hadn't been content? Had he even been happy when he was with Hayleigh? In the beginning, he must have been. But lately? The people he'd got to know in Leeds were her friends. They'd been to all her favourite places, done all her favourite things. Somewhere along the line, he'd stopped doing the simple stuff that he liked — walking along the canal, going to the cinema, the drawing class. How had that happened?

When had he morphed from laid back and happy Vinnie, into the man most likely to marry Hayleigh Stanhope? And when had that stopped being good enough for her?

He thought about the press of Tracey lying on top of him. Of the intense desire to kiss her. Another second and he couldn't have stopped himself. He stamped down the small niggle of guilt. He had nothing to feel guilty about. He was single now. Except, he hadn't been single for long. He sighed. That wouldn't be fair on Tracey. He shot another look at her across the room. She seemed so closed and private when he first met her and now she'd loosened up towards him. She clearly didn't open up to people very often. Her friendship was a privilege. It would be a terrible thing to abuse it.

She looked across and caught his eye. He felt a stab of embarrassment that he had been staring at her. She slid off her bar stool and came over.

"Hi." She sat down opposite him. "How're you feeling? Have you recovered?"

For a second he didn't know what she was talking about, then remembered. "Yes, I've recovered thanks. Now I'm merely exhausted."

"But it's a good sort of tired," she said. "If you know what I mean?"

Weirdly, he did. It was a hard earned tiredness that came from physical exertion rather than the brain ache tiredness that he normally battled with. It was oddly refreshing. "I do know what you mean. I guess going to the gym isn't really a substitute for getting out into the fresh air."

"Hmm." She pushed her hair back and tucked it behind her ear. "I'm not totally convinced. It was nice of you to help," she said.

"It's nice to be useful... and to be appreciated, I guess," he said. "Lawyers don't always get that."

"I guess not. App developers on the other hand, either get ignored or get fawned over, depending on how well their product is doing."

"Which one are you?" He didn't really know much about apps, although he assumed they were harder to make than they looked. He'd done a few contracts for clients, but those had been fairly straightforward and didn't require him to know about the work itself.

"I've been both," she said. "Right now, I'm pretty much old news. It's a fast turnover in the tech world."

He watched her face. When she spoke about her work there was a certain bitterness. A narrowing of the eyes. It couldn't be nice being shoved out of the limelight. "I'm sorry."

She frowned. "What for?"

"That... um... you feel you're old news. I assume that was a touchy subject."

"Oh that. No. Not really. I'm not comfortable with attention."

"So what's annoyed you about work? Is your app not selling well?"

She laughed. "On the contrary. It was selling so well, it got bought out. The trouble is, it's not mine anymore. I don't have control. It's drifting away."

"And it was your baby." That was it. "That must be hard. To build something up from nothing and then watch someone else mess with it."

"Yeah." She looked down at her hands. "I'm sure I'll get used to it." Again that vulnerability, hidden under the prickly attitude that she wore like a cloak.

His heart went out to her. "You know," he said. "A patent attorney friend of mine says that she always sees the same clients over and over because if you're the sort of person who invents one thing, you've got the sort of mind that will keep doing it over and over again. So if you made one app that someone wanted to buy, you'll probably do it again."

She narrowed her eyes. "Have you any idea what is involved in writing an app? It's not just a flash of inspiration that's needed you know."

"I didn't mean that. I meant that if you had that sort of mind—" She wasn't looking any less annoyed, so he gave up. "Never mind. It's probably the tiredness talking."

She closed her eyes and breathed out slowly. "Sorry," she said. "I'm sorry. I'm just... tired, like you say. I get snappy when I'm tired."

He smiled. "I'll remember that. I shall stay out of your reach for the rest of the evening. Well, beyond kneeing distance anyway."

Her face went pink. "I really am very sorry about that. It was an accident. I didn't mean to."

He laughed. "I know. It's fine. No harm done."

The phone on the bar rang, prompting a cheer from the room.

"Phones are back up, then," said someone. "Now we can phone council and find out when they're going to come dig us out."

Angie picked up the phone and spoke to whoever it was. She explained, loudly, that no one was seriously hurt, but there were elderly people who needed help sooner rather than later thank you.

Vinnie and Tracey exchanged glances. They had both seen how frightened some people had been by the sudden communications blackout. It seemed that the lack of a telephone line was almost more frightening than the thought of freezing or starving to death.

After a few more minutes, Angie hung up. She turned to face the room. "Snow plough's coming in tomorrow."

Another cheer. Someone shouted out, "That means we'll be able to get home to put us glad rags on in time for the Christmas do."

"Is the do still on?" said someone else.

"Of course it is," said Angie. "I've bought all the food. It'll take more than a bloody snow storm to stop my party."

This time the cheer was full throated.

Vinnie cheered along with everyone else. Why not. A Christmas party, what could show spirit and defiance better than that? Once the roads were cleared, he could get back to the cottage and get a clean shirt and a jumper to wear. He ran a hand over his face. A shave wouldn't go amiss either.

He became aware that Tracey was looking at him. He raised an eyebrow at her. "What?"

"Are you coming to the party?"

"Of course."

Her smile was a pure delight. "Cool," she said. "I'll see you there." She stood up and went across to do something behind the bar.

Vinnie realised he was smiling after her. Oh dear. Whatever it was he was feeling, he was clearly giving off interested vibes. He needed to watch that. Tracey was a nice person. He didn't want to mess around with her feelings. Not while he was so confused by his own.

TRACEY ALL BUT CRAWLED up the stairs to bed, she was that tired. Angie had kept the bar open as usual, despite everyone being totally worn out by the day's efforts. It took an almost superhuman effort to clean her teeth and get changed before she dropped face down onto the bed. Vinnie had gone to bed by eight pm, sensible guy. She wished she could have done the same.

She rolled over onto her back and thought of that moment in the snow. She had intended only to push him into the snow bank, but she had misjudged it, as usual and her momentum had taken her over as well. His face had been so close. She could smell his deodorant and feel the warm brush of his breath. He had incredible eyes. Deep brown with a hint of black at the edges. When his gaze held hers, she'd felt completely detached from her surroundings. Everything else disappeared until there was just her and him - the caress of his breath, the heat of his body, the beating of his heart under her palm. She had wanted to kiss him so badly it made her chest ache. But then she'd kneed him in the groin instead. She groaned. Smooth, Tracey. Smooth.

It was a wonder he was still talking to her! She'd expected awkwardness. He'd done something playful and fun and she'd responded like a nutcase... and yet he didn't seem fazed by it. Even after the knee to the soft parts.

She sighed. This was how it went. She didn't often meet men she was attracted to. That was part of the problem with being a girl in a man's field. Oh, there were more and more techie women now, but they all seemed to have got themselves sorted out so that they didn't feel the need to run and hide when someone, anyone, tried to talk to them. She'd got over that by being prickly. The 'don't talk to me, I'm a bitch' vibe worked incredibly well. Giselle was the approachable one in the team. You only needed one. The only problem was, when she actually wanted to drop the guard, she realised she didn't know what to do instead.

"I'm so broken," she whispered into the empty room. "Ugh." She let her thoughts drift back to the few seconds when she'd been that close to kissing Vinnie. So close. Still imagining how it could have gone differently, she drifted off to sleep.

Chapter 12

The pub was packed solid with noise and tinsel. Tracey felt terribly out of place in her plain red t-shirt. She had intended to wear the one that said 'bah, humbug' on it, but one look at her aunt's face had been enough to make her go change. Everyone else seemed to have gone completely mad. Harriet was wearing a ridiculous sparkly dress and earrings that flashed red and green. In fairness, she wasn't the only one wearing LED infused jewellery, Sue and her friend Margie were wearing matching Christmas pudding earrings that twinkled. Those who weren't wearing tasteless jewellery were wearing tasteless Christmas jumpers.

Tracey had never understood the Christmas jumper thing. Giselle had explained the concept of 'so bad it's good' to her, but she still didn't get it. Why would you buy a jumper that you could only wear for one week in the year? And why would you choose for it to be something you wouldn't be seen dead in at any other time?

She made her way to the buffet table and helped herself to some canapes.

"Hello," said a voice behind her. She turned to find Vinnie. He was wearing a jumper. It had a reindeer motif on it. Tracey pulled a face.

Vinnie looked down. "Um. Yeah. Just getting into the spirit of things."

"Uh huh."

"I see you're not... getting into the spirit, I mean."

"No. I don't really get the point."

"There isn't really a point, is there?" He helped himself to a turkey and cranberry vol-au-vent. "It's just a bit of fun."

"Are we talking about the jumpers and the godawful jewellery? Or the whole of Christmas?"

"Oh Christmas has a point. It's there to remind you what it's like to be in close proximity with your family, so that you're really pleased to get back to your own place. Mind you, my family don't do that, so perhaps I don't appreciate my own space as much as I could." He pointed to the canapes. "These are really good."

"I thought you get on well with your family. Perhaps the reason for that is the absence of forced Christmas fun?"

"Oh, we do forced festive fun," said Vinnie. "Just not on Christmas day. We used to, but then we kids grew up and now my parents go down to London to an annual Christmas do. They wouldn't miss it for anything short of a crisis."

Tracey shuddered.

"Oh come on." He looked around. "It's not that bad."

"It's not. I'm just not good with parties." They were tiring and there were too many people. Too many things to change focus between. Give it an hour and she'd be fighting a headache.

"Is it because of your eyes?"

"Sort of," she said. "It's hard to tell which parts are me being antisocial because of my eyes... and which bits are because I'm just being me."

Vinnie didn't say anything for a minute. Tracey felt his scrutiny and felt her skin prickling with her awareness of him. Could he see what she was thinking?

Finally, he said "Perhaps your eyes have shaped the way you view the world in more ways than one." And Tracey knew she was lost. No one had understood her so well, so quickly before. Was it possible to fall in love in the course of 48 hours?

Vinnie, who could have no idea what she was feeling, popped the canapé in his mouth. "Mmm. This is good." He picked up another and offered it to her. "Try it."

Tracey hesitated. It was such an intimate gesture, but Vinnie didn't seem to think anything of it. Her face heated up as she leaned in and took a bite, a small one so that she could be sure that she didn't bite him or something awful like that. She chewed and nodded her head, even though she barely noticed the taste of it. Now he had half a canape left in his hand. She lifted her paper plate up, so that he could deposit it there.

"Vinnie! You came!" Harriet appeared out of the throng. "Merry Christmas!" She placed a firm kiss on his cheek, leaving a red lipstick mark. "Come and dance."

Vinnie threw Tracey an apologetic glance over his shoulder as he abandoned his plate and was dragged in the direction of the tiny but busy dancefloor. Tracey sighed. This sort of thing always happened. If Giselle were here, she'd help her sort Harriet out, but Giselle was in America and it looked like Harriet was going to win. Arse-biscuits.

Tracey sighed again and went to see if Angie needed any help.

Angie was glad to see her and immediately gave her a list of tasks. As Tracey went about her business, she tried not to stare at Harriet and Vinnie dancing to cheesy Christmas tunes. She had no idea what a good dancer looked like, but Vinnie seemed to be throwing himself into the dancing with gusto.

After a few dances, she saw Vinnie extricate himself and go over to talk to some of the men he'd been out working with the day before. Much to her surprise, she felt her own shoulders relax a little. Was she so jealous that she couldn't stand to watch Vinnie dancing with someone? Yes. Yes she was. In that case, she needed to do something about it. Maybe she could ask him out. How did one ask someone out? She didn't know how to flirt. She certainly couldn't blatantly throw herself at him the way Harriet seemed to be doing. Anyway, Harriet didn't seem to be having much luck, so why would she fare any better?

She thought of the moment lying in the snow... and the few seconds of connection before he'd fed her a canape. There was definitely a something...

"If you want to go talk to him, I can manage here, you know," said Angie.

Tracey jumped. "What?"

Angie smiled. "I'm just saying that he's only booked the cottage until tomorrow lunchtime. If you're going to do anything about how you feel... best to do it tonight."

"I don't... I—"

"Go on," her aunt nudged her. "You like him. He keeps looking at you. Go talk to him. See where it goes. Or that slapper Harriet will pounce on the poor lad."

"Only if he wants to be pounced on, though," said Tracey. "He's a grown man. I'm sure he could turn her down if he wasn't interested."

"You don't know Harriet," her aunt said, darkly.

They both turned to look at Vinnie, who saw them looking and raised a quizzical eyebrow.

There was a squeal from the other side of the pub. Someone had held up a bunch of mistletoe. Harriet moved towards it like a homing missile.

"Uh oh. Here's trouble," said someone.

Angie practically pushed Tracey out from behind the bar. "Go."

Tracey stood there, staring. She saw Harriet grab the mistletoe and look around the pub. Someone nudged Vinnie and pointed. He turned. His eyes widened and his smile dropped.

If she was going to do anything, it had to be now. If Harriet got her claws into Vinnie, there was a real risk that Tracey would never see him again. In this microcosm, for this short time, she had been given an opportunity. She couldn't waste it.

Tracey marched across the pub. The two women converged on Vinnie.

Harriet got there a split second before Tracey did. She waved the mistletoe. "Hey Vinnie, look what I found." She held it up above his head.

Vinnie gave Tracey a desperate look.

"Ooh, mistletoe," said Tracey. She stepped in front of Harriet, put a hand behind Vinnie's neck, pulled him down and kissed him. There was a second of surprised stasis and Vinnie kissed her back. She moved her thumb along the side of his neck and there was a gratifying hitch to his breath. His hands rested on her hips, not moving, but holding firm. Her blood thundered around her body. She felt powerful, incandescent.

The rest of the world disappeared. It was just her, and him and the kiss to end all kisses.

When they finally drew apart there was applause and wolf whistles. Tracey felt like she'd gone up in flames. Vinnie's hands were still on her hips, probably just as well because she wasn't totally sure she could trust her legs.

Vinnie held her gaze, not smiling. There was a beat, two, of silence. Then he breathed out. "Wow."

And just like that, her world went mad. She wanted him, so badly that her hands shook. "What do you say we bust out of this joint?" she said, in his ear.

"Lead on."

She took his hand marched out, ignoring the catcalls from the audience. She didn't stop or look back until she'd led him all the way up the stairs to the top of the house, to her room. As soon as they got in the door, he kissed her again; urgent, hungry kisses. Tracey kissed him back. His hand reached under her t-shirt and her bare skin caught fire under his palm. She pushed him backwards towards the bed. A step at a time.

He banged into something so hard that their teeth knocked together. She'd forgotten all about the sloping eaves. Vinnie dropped onto the bed. "Ow."

She sat down next to him and turned on the bedside light. He was rubbing his head. The moment was totally ruined. "Are you okay?"

He nodded slowly. "Being with you," he said solemnly. "Is a really painful experience."

"I'm so sorry." The tide of happiness and triumph was turning into anger and humiliation. Tears prickled at her eyes. "I'm such a klutz. I should have–" A tear, fat and wet and embarrassing, escaped down her cheek. Not only was she a total disaster as seduction, she was now going to ruin it further by crying on him.

"Hey." Vinnie put his arm around her and wiped the tear away with his thumb. "I already knew you were a klutz. It's part of your weird charm."

It was such a preposterous comment that it made her smile. "What charm?"

"You know, the charm," he said. "That thing you've got that makes me want to do this." He kissed her, very gently, his lips lingering lightly on hers.

"Oh," she said. Her feelings were so confused now that she didn't know what they were. What she did know was that she wanted more of him. "I like you," she said. "I'm just not very good at these things."

Vinnie gave a little shrug. "I'm not so great at these things either," he said. "But when you kissed me earlier... I have never, ever been kissed like that before." He kicked off his shoes and lay down on her bed. He pulled her down until she was lying partially on top of him. "I like you too, Tracey," he said. "And I really, really want to get to know you better. Just ... be gentle with me."

She giggled and kicked off her own shoes. She lay next to him and ran her fingers through his hair. "You're insane."

In response he kissed her again and this time, there was nothing in world that could stop them.

Chapter 13

Vinnie woke up in the dark. There was someone asleep on his arm. Tracey. He smiled into the darkness. She made him feel... happy. It was a simple sort of happiness as though she was a tonic that he'd been needing all his life. He shifted his weight so that he could tweak the curtains a bit. He had to move carefully, not only because he didn't want to wake her, but because they were in a single bed. One false move and he could add falling out of bed to his list of Tracey related accidents.

Dawn was streaking pink across the sky. The soft light fell on Tracey's sleeping face. Without her glasses she looked delicate and young. Vulnerable. He didn't want to ever let her go. All his concerns about being on the rebound had vanished the minute she kissed him. Nothing he had felt for Hayleigh compared to the head rush of being with Tracey. Except, she worked in London, he lived in Leeds. There were fast trains ... and the internet. It wasn't ideal, but it was doable. He shifted his weight again and tried to extricate his arm.

Tracey started and eyes flew open. She stared at him like a frightened animal for a second, before her body relaxed. "Vinnie."

"Tracey." He grinned, took her hand in his and kissed it. "Morning."

She smiled back, a satisfied, sated kind of smile that made him want to kiss her all over again. Then she stretched.

"No, don't do th—"

Too late. She moved her body into the stretch and he toppled out of the bed.

He lay on the floor, tangled in the duvet which had come with him, and rolled his eyes. It had to happen.

Her head appeared over the side of the bed. Her red and black hair all over the place. "Sorry."

"I'm getting used to it." He sat up. "Actually, I need to get dressed and go up to the cottage anyway. I'm supposed to clear out by lunchtime."

"Oh." Her face fell. "Do you have to go?"

He pulled up his knees and rested his arms on them. "I promised my Mum I'd be home for dinner. I could pretend we're still snowed in..."

She slid down onto the floor next to him. He pulled her to him and wrapped the duvet around them both. "It's only a short term fix though," he said. "I would really like to see you again... if that's okay with you."

The smile she gave him put a glow in his chest. "It's definitely okay with me."

"Excellent." He moved closer to kiss her.

"Oh wait, there's one thing."

He leaned back again and raised his eyebrows.

"I can't go out with someone without knowing their name. If you're not really called Vincent, what IS your real name?"

He grinned. "Vinodh. It means 'he who enjoys' ..."

She gave it more thought that he'd expected. "It suits you," she said, finally.

"Great. Now can I kiss you?"

She threw her arms around him and did it for him.

Chapter 14

Tracey sat in the car, working. She'd agreed to do a patch for Nifty Gift It's new owners as a one-off. The Wi-Fi was just another reason why she liked Bob's cars. She was so busy with her laptop that she didn't notice they'd stopped until Bob said, "This is the place, miss. Do you know the code to let us in past the barrier?"

She looked up and took a moment to surface into the real world. "No idea," she said. "Just a sec. I'll call Vinnie."

He picked up after a couple of rings. "Tracey! Where are you?"

"Outside your gate thing. Can you let us in?"

"I'll buzz you in. I'm in Ariadne block, the third one down. I'll come down and meet you."

As the barrier rose, Tracey relayed the information to Bob. It was February and it was dark outside. She hadn't seen Vinnie since Christmas, but they'd spoken to each other by phone and Skype so much, that it was almost as though they'd never been apart. She peered out at the blocks of modern apartments and felt a flutter of excitement at the idea of seeing him again. She hadn't told anyone except Giselle about him and Giselle had teased her about having an online relationship with a man she'd actually met.

Her phone rang. She checked the caller ID and clicked her tongue. It was the agent who was trying to find a tenant for her flat. She'd shown someone round earlier, maybe these people were interested in the renting the place. Tracey sighed and took the call. Bob stopped the car at the entrance to one of the blocks.

It took her a couple of minutes to sort out the phone call. She hung up and scrambled out of the car. Bob had taken her bags out for her.

"Tracey?"

She turned. Vinnie stood in the light from the building. He was evidently still in his work clothes, his shirt open at the collar. He looked... amazing. The butterflies in her stomach went mad. This man. This beautiful man... was *her* man. It was almost too good to be true.

He was looking at the car, a small frown between his brows.

"I'll come pick you on Monday morning then, miss." Bob touched his cap. She wished he wouldn't do that. It made her look like some sort of moneyed doyenne.

"Yes please. Have a good weekend, Bob."

Bob's gaze flicked to Vinnie and back to her. "You too."

Vinnie watched the car drive away and turned to Tracey. "Hello." He leaned across and kissed her cheek awkwardly. "Here. Let me take that bag."

She followed him and was nervous again. This had happened on and off the whole time she was on the way up. Would things still be the same, now that they were out of the Trewton Royd bubble? They'd been talking over Skype and messaging each other for the past few weeks, while busily getting on with their real lives off screen. With Valentine's Day coming up, it seemed the ideal opportunity to meet up again. In real life. He'd offered to come to her, but she'd insisted on coming up.

She couldn't bear the thought of having to go out in London. Besides, there were things she needed to do in Leeds.

Now that Bob had gone off and left her there, the doubts returned. Butterflies in her stomach. Her throat was tight. What if the magic had worn off? What if he'd changed his mind? In the lift, they stood side by side.

Vinnie leaned his head back against the side of the lift and said, "So... when you said you were getting a lift up... you actually meant a chauffeur driven limo?"

That was the other thing. She still hadn't mentioned about the money. She hadn't wanted him to know at first, because she wanted him to like her as she was. And then it was too late to tell him without raising awkward questions. "Um... yeah. The train is... difficult sometimes."

"Yes, but a chauffeur driven limo? What are you made of money?" He didn't look annoyed, just puzzled.

"Well, actually. There's something I need to tell you."

He turned to face her. "Don't tell me. You're a millionaire." He grinned. When she didn't laugh, the grin faded. The lift stopped and the doors opened. "You're not?" he said. "Are you?"

"Are we getting out?" She stepped out. He followed her, looking baffled.

"I knew you'd made some money. But when they said how much the company sold for, I assumed a lot of that was taken up by shareholders. Were there no shareholders? Was it really just you and Giselle?"

She nodded. He must have Googled her. Of course. She had Googled him.

"I'm impressed. Well done, Tracey." He started walking down the corridor.

She followed him. "You're not weirded out?"

He stopped at a door and fished a key out of his pocket. "No. Should I be? I mean, it's impressive, but you earned it." He guided her in, his hand touching her back gently. She felt a thrill at the contact. She wasn't sure what reaction she'd expected, but unruffled acceptance was just perfect. She should have known that Vinnie would take it in his stride.

"This is *chez moi*," he said. They were in the hallway of a small flat. Music spilled out an open doorway to the side.

"Come through to the kitchen," he said. "I'm making lasagne."

The kitchen, to one side of the open plan living/dining room, was small and looked like a bomb had hit it. There was stuff everywhere.

"Wow. This looks ... complicated," said Tracey.

"It's not, really." He grated cheese into a bowl. "I just ... tend to spread out a bit when I'm cooking." He put the cheese down and pulled a corkscrew out of a drawer. "Would you mind getting the wine?"

There were two glasses already out. She poured the drinks carefully. "This is a bit more fancy than a pint in the Trewton Arms." She pushed his glass towards him.

Vinnie picked up the glass. "Nicely done," he said, nodding towards the clean work surface. "Not a drop of spillage."

"I'm a lot better now that I'm not so stressed." Which was true. She still had to concentrate, but it was easier now that she wasn't so tired all the time.

"That's great." He returned to his cooking.

Tracey leaned against the worktop and watched him move. She could watch him for hours. The way he moved was something that Skype could never convey. What else was there that didn't translate over the distance? Again, she felt a twist of fear. Oh please don't let this get messed up. She had never wanted to be with anyone as much as she wanted to be with Vinnie. Please, please, please.

He finished sprinkling cheese on the pasta and put the dish in the oven. "There," he said. "It's going to be... bloody ages before it's done." He washed his hands and ran his fingers through his hair. "It was meant to be all sorted by the time you got here, but I was late leaving work." He came and stood facing her. Took a sip of wine. They looked at each other.

"Well, this is weird," said Tracey.

He smiled. "It is a bit, isn't it? You look different," he said.

"It'll be the fact that I'm not wearing a bazillion jumpers and my nose isn't bright red," she said, a little more sharply than she'd intended. Old habits died hard.

He touched her cheek, as though moving a strand of hair off it. "You've changed the colour in your hair," he said. "That's all."

"Oh. Yeah. I thought it was time to try shocking pink." She finally looked up to meet his eyes. He was still gorgeous. That hadn't changed. He stroked her cheek again and the butterflies in her stomach went crazy. That hadn't changed either.

"You know what else is weird." He moved closer.

"What?" It was getting hard to think.

"You've been here ten minutes and haven't beaten me up once." Closer, closer.

By the time he kissed her, she was smiling. It was a gentle kiss to begin with. Light and reassuring. Tracey leaned into him, the tension leaving her. She wrapped her arms around his neck and kissed him back. The kiss changed. Deepened. Now filled with wanting. Nothing had changed. She still wanted him and, heaven knows, he still wanted her. Thank goodness.

They finally drew apart. He held her to him. "I've missed you," he said. "Talking on Skype is great, but it's not the same." He kissed the corner of her mouth. "Being so far apart sucks."

"Actually, Vinnie, there's something else I wanted to tell you." She put her hands on his chest and leaned away so that she could see him. His shirt was lovely and thick, but she could feel the heat of him through it.

"Don't tell me. You want me to be your virginal secretary," he said. "I'm not sure I can do that, Tracey."

She punched him gently in the chest.

"At last. The beating up. Now I'm on familiar territory."

"Shut up for a minute," she said. "I'm trying to tell you that I'm thinking of moving up to Leeds."

He dropped his hands to her waist. "Really?" A huge grin rose on his face. "How? When?"

"Well, I've just found a tenant for my flat ... so in the next couple of weeks. I'll need to go flat hunting here this weekend, if that's okay with you."

"But Tracey, all your work contacts. The prospects."

"They can find me just as easily here. I tend to do everything online anyway and I can do that from anywhere. Anyway, I've got an idea for a new app. You were right about the ideas." His grin was catching. Now she was beaming too. "So... is that okay with you?"

"Is that okay with me?" He laughed. "I love you, you idiot. Of course it's okay with me."

Emotion rose through her body. He loved her. Unexpected tears made him blurry. "Oh Vinnie." She threw her arms around his neck and buried her face in his shoulder. He wrapped his arms around her and held her close to him, her body pressed against his, his arms warm around her. "I can't believe this is real," she said into his shoulder.

"It's real." He drew back so that he could tilt her face up to look at him. "I've never been more sure of anything before. When I'm with you, I feel like I'm a better version of me. I don't know how I'd be without you."

Tears escaped down her face. "I don't know how to be without you either."

He wiped away the tears and took her face in his hands. "Awesome." He kissed her and she kissed him back, her hands pressed against his chest. The kiss became more urgent. She slid her fingers in between the buttons on his shirt and felt the hot skin underneath.

He made an appreciative noise in his throat and scooped her up.

"But the lasagne..." Her protest was half-hearted at best.

"Ages," he said firmly, and carried her off to his bedroom.

The End

THANK YOU FOR READING *Snowed In*. If you enjoyed it, please leave a review at your favourite book retailer.

WHAT TO READ NEXT

If you enjoyed *Snowed In* why not try the rest of the Trewton Royd series. They can all be read as standalone stories:

BELONGING – Harriet is still grieving when her late lover's teenage daughter turns up on her doorstep. Can helping the teenager move on help Harriet too?

Christmas for Commitmentphobes – Lara is too busy for romance and Tilly is not the sort to settle down. Can being forced to spend Christmas in the Trewton Arms change their minds?

That Holiday in France – Just when Ellie decides she doesn't need a man to complete her, she meets Ash. But does she like him enough to give up her independence?

Want even *more* Christmas?

Join my mailing list to be the first to hear about my new books and to get exclusive behind the scenes information that other people don't get to see. You also get:

- A FREE copy of *Girl At Christmas* – a Smart Girls novella.
- An exclusive short story that you can't get anywhere else.

GET THE FREE BOOK ON my website www.rhodabaxter.com

OR GO DIRECTLY TO https://www.subscribepage.com/landSnowedIn

Remember Harriet from the corner shop?

Find out why she drinks in Belonging. The next book in the series.

Belonging

By Rhoda Baxter

Chapter 1

It was so dark, it felt like the middle of the night and when Harriet slammed the taxi door, it sounded like a gunshot in the deserted village street. There would be curtains twitching in a minute. The only place with lights on was the bakery where Sue would be at work on her bread already. Sanctimonious cow. Sue had caught Harriet doing the walk of shame at 4 in the morning many a time and would always make some comment. Imagine what she'd have to say about her going out midweek.

Harriet stepped with exaggerated care up to the door at the side of 'her' corner shop, two doors along the street from the bakery. Her feet were already numb in these stupid shoes and it wouldn't do to twist her ankle as well. Angling her body away from the street light, so that she could see the keyhole, she had a couple of stabs before she got the key in the lock and stumbled in.

After the darkness outside, the light in the narrow hallway was blinding. She covered her eyes and peered through her fingers. The stairs seemed to pulse ahead of her. Urgh. Not good. The hangover was going to be brutal tomorrow ... well, later today, technically. She had to open the shop in five hours.

She went up the stairs on her hands and knees, pausing at the top to take off her heels. There was another door at the top. Harriet unlocked that door too, took a deep breath and pushed it open.

The flat was exactly as she'd left it. Fairly neat. Fairly tidy. Totally empty, apart from her. She chucked her shoes into the basket in the corner and padded to the kitchen where she got herself a glass of water. Of course it was empty. What had she expected? That he would miraculously be there waiting for her? And what if he had? What would he have said to find her staggering home smelling of booze and smoke and some random guy she'd pulled in a nightclub?

Harriet gulped down another mouthful of cold water. He'd be horrified and upset, that's what. There would be tears and remorse and she'd feel awful. But she'd happily live through that … just to see him again for five minutes.

Oh balls. This was what she'd gone out to avoid. This … yearning. She didn't have any more booze in the house. There was wine downstairs, in the shop, but she had enough sanity left to know that was out of bounds. Tears leaked down her cold cheeks. Harriet wove her way to the bedroom and, still dressed, curled up under the duvet and gave into the sadness until she fell asleep.

WHEN THE ALARM WENT off four hours later, Harriet smacked it to snooze and uncurled, slowly, so that she didn't shatter herself into pieces. Ow. Ow. There was a band of pain around her head. She hauled herself up until she was vaguely sitting up, found the water and ibuprofen she'd put out on the bedside cabinet before she went out and gulped it down. She reset the alarm and sank back under the duvet. One snooze and she'd go downstairs. All she had to do was sort the papers.

SITTING AT HIS COMPUTER Tim stared at his inbox. 212 messages. How was that even possible? He'd wrestled it down to less than 20 before going home the night before. He rubbed his eyes and briefly considered deleting the whole lot, just to see what happened. But no. That would be irresponsible. One of his graduate students might have emailed him something that was actually important. At least he could get rid of all the university administrative emails telling him about when scheduled computer system updates or road closures. He sighed and started to work through them, trying to prioritise the onslaught so that he didn't get buried in it.

His mobile phone rang. He pulled it out and looked at the caller ID. Mel. Crap. He looked at his inbox and considered ignoring the call. She would only call back. He'd already had three missed calls from her that morning. She was nothing if not persistent, his twin sister.

He sank into his chair before he answered it. This was not going to be easy. Discussions with Mel never were.

"There you are," she said, by way of greeting. "I've been trying to get hold of you for days. Don't you ever answer your phone?"

"Hi, Mel. I'm fine, thanks. You?"

She clicked her tongue. "I know you're fine, Tim. I friended you on Facebook, remember?"

Had she? Oh bugger. He'd forgotten about that. He'd only friended her so that he could keep up with what his niece Niamh was doing. Of course it meant that Mel could see what he was up to too.

"Anyway," said Mel. "I'm calling because I need a huge favour."

There it was. Straight to the point. Although, on reflection, it saved a lot of time not beating about the bush. "I dunno, Mel, I'm really busy at the moment."

"I know you are, Tim. I wouldn't have called you if it wasn't urgent."

Tim sighed. Fair enough. She was pretty self-sufficient. She had a husband and friends to lean on, anyway. "What do you want, Mel?"

There was a tiny pause. "You know how Alex and I are going away on a retreat in Scotland in a week's time."

"Yes ..."

"And Niamh was going to her godmother's place while we were away."

Tim closed his eyes and rubbed at the headache that was gathering on his forehead. He had a feeling he knew what was coming. "Mel, I can't look after Niamh. I'm completely snowed under with work. I have deadlines coming out of my ears and there's a new cohort of students arriving in two weeks. I—"

"Oh, Tim, please? Niamh's godmother has broken her leg and she can't manage Niamh on top of that."

"What is there to manage with Niamh? She's fourteen. She only needs an adult to be around. She doesn't need spoon-feeding."

"Exactly! You could keep an eye on her in the evenings and make sure she gets something to eat. She's ever such a nice girl, she'll be no bother. She'll be spending the day at holiday club anyway, so you don't need to worry about her during the day."

"Mel ..." he said. But his heart wasn't in it. Mel would keep trying to persuade him and he didn't have the energy to argue with her. She always won. Besides, he liked Niamh. Scratch that, he loved Niamh. He had spent a lot of time with her when Mel split up with her first husband. For a time, he had lived in his sister's house, acting as in-house babysitter while Mel sorted out mortgages and lawyers and got shot of Niamh's father Richard. Tim and Niamh had become very close as a result. Later, he'd been there to keep Mel calm while Richard took Niamh away on his access days. He and Mel argued and bickered, but if she ever needed him, he would be there. He would never to say no to her. And they both knew it.

"Please, please, please. You'll get to hang out with Niamh without me around. I've asked everyone else I can think of. You're my last hope."

"Oh thanks." He leaned back in his chair. "Can't you cancel your trip?"

"You know I can't. It's taken me so long to arrange this. You know how hard it would be to get Alex to take time off again." There was a tell-tale wobble in her voice. He recognised the latent panic in it. He knew what it meant. Mel's second marriage had been slowly deteriorating – according to Mel. Alex worked too hard and his initial adoration had faded to something more mundane. Mel was feeling ignored ... and Mel hated being ignored. Tim had initially wondered if Mel was just being a drama queen, but he now knew that she was genuinely worried.

"Okay," he said. "I'll do it. I'll come and stay at yours, but I'll have to work in the evenings. Niamh will pretty much have to entertain herself."

Mel gave a little laugh. "She'll be fine with that. All she ever wants to do is sit on Skype to her friends or watch Netflix."

Tim smiled. Teenagers. Then he remembered all that had happened in Niamh's life in the past few months. "How is she?" he asked. "Is she okay?"

Mel sighed. "Yeah. She seems to be ... getting on with things. She still bursts into tears from time to time, but not so often now. Mostly, she worries about friends and hairstyles and the usual stuff now."

"Oh good. And how about you?"

"Well, I'm not exactly upset about Richard dying," she said, too quickly. "I've got enough to worry about keeping my marriage to Alex alive."

Tim frowned. Despite her brusque manner, he could feel the worry that bubbled underneath. "How's that going?"

Mel sighed. "In all honesty, I don't know. A fortnight in a retreat, with no computers or mobiles, might get Alex away from his computer long enough to sort things out ... or it might just prove that we can't be fixed. I don't know."

For a few seconds there was silence. The years fell away and they were six again. Tim, with scrubbed clean hands and paper face mask, was sitting on Mel's hospital bed, playing Scrabble with the hospital's special set that smelled of disinfectant. He'd had a brilliant six letter word all lined up, but one look at his sister sitting there with tubes coming out of her nose and wrist, and he'd ignored it in favour of a lousy three letter one. He'd let her win then and had been letting her win ever since.

There was no point fighting it. It was just a waste of precious time. "You go to your retreat," Tim said, quietly. "I'll keep an eye on Niamh."

"Thanks Tim. You're ... well, thank you."

Tim laughed. "The words you're looking for are 'you're awesome.'"

She clicked her tongue. "Oh don't you start. You hardly inspire awe." Her voice softened, as though she was about to laugh too. "But yes, thank you." A beat passed. "Can you come round at about four on Friday? I'll run you through everything before I head off." And just like that, they were back to business.

"Sure. I'll see you Friday."

He was smiling when he hung up. He could take a bit of time off to hang out with his niece at the weekend. It had been weeks since he'd last seen her. With a jolt, he realised it had actually been months. Time flies. He opened his email and looked at the 5 messages that had come in while he was on the phone. This mountain of work would still be there, whether he took the weekend off or not. Maybe some of it would even go away. Maybe doing something different wasn't such a bad idea.

This is the end of sample chapter. To continue reading, buy Belonging now.

HOW DO YOU KNOW WHEN *it's time to let go?*

Hiding away in a tiny Yorkshire village, Harriet is grieving for her lost lover. His family won't talk to her and she can't move on from his death. All this changes when his daughter, Niamh, turns up on her doorstep, needing a sympathetic ear.

Tim thinks Harriet broke up his sister's marriage. His sister's enemies are his enemies. When his frantic search for his runaway niece takes him to Harriet's house, all he wants to do is get away.

As they work together to console Niamh and get her home safely, Tim and Harriet become increasingly attracted to each other.

But with attraction comes guilt.

Can they overcome their respective loyalties and give in to love?

---

1. http://www.books2read.com/u/bzPAZq

Other Books by Rhoda Baxter

Trewton Royd small town romance novellas - All can be read as standalone stories

Pat's Pantry - short story

Snowed In

Belonging

Christmas for Commitmentphobes

That Holiday in France

SMART GIRLS SERIES -All can be read as standalone stories

Girl On The Run – nominated for Joan Hessayon award

Girl Having A Ball - nominated for Romantic Comedy of the Year 2017 RoNA awards

Girl In Trouble

Girl At Christmas - novella

SHORT STORIES:

Kisschase - A collection of six short stories

The Truth About the Other Guy

One Night in Shining Armour

BOOKS WRITTEN AS JEEVANI Charika

Christmas At The Palace – shortlisted for the Emma prize and The Pink Heart Soc reader choice

This Stolen Life – Longlisted for *Guardian* Not The Booker Prize

A Convenient Marriage – shortlisted for RoNA contemporary romantic novel award 2020

Acknowledgments

The Trewton Royd stories came about because I wrote a short story called Pat's Pantry and, for some reason, I found that the voices in it were all from West Yorkshire. When I was a teenager, I lived in village in between Halifax and Huddersfield. It was far less rural than Trewton Royd, but probably as picturesque. For the first few weeks, I couldn't understand a word anyone said, although they understood me perfectly. Once I 'got me ear in', I loved the Yorkshire accent.

I wanted to spend more time in that world, so I wrote a Christmas novella about it. The general word in publishing circles was that nobody wanted to read contemporary novels set in Yorkshire. People wanted Scotland, Ireland or Cornwall. Which meant that I knew I had to self-publish this novella. Since I've been wanting to write a book with a Sri Lankan hero for a while (and again, was told it would be hard to sell), I threw that in too. So the story of Vinnie and his ridiculous romantic cottage for one was born. Tracey was inspired by two women entrepreneurs that I saw on a reality TV show about tech entrepreneurs. They were amazing women. They had just sold their company for a substantial amount of money and were moving on to new things. I made Tracey a lot more geeky than either of those ladies because I like geeky people. I also quite like the idea of having a streak of red in your hair (my hair doesn't hold on to dye very well – buy me a drink and ask me what happened when I tried to dye my hair purple).

Thank yous – actually, these ones will be pretty short. To Jen Hicks for making me write something else set in Trewton, to Kate Johnson and Ruth Long who did the edits and proof-read and said nice things about the book. To the amazing Milly Johnson (fellow Yorkshire person) who took the time to read it and give me a cover quote! As always, to my husband and kids for putting up with my disappearing into my head from time to time.

Lastly, thank you to you, for buying this book so that I can afford to keep writing more.

About the Author

Rhoda Baxter writes contemporary romances with heart and a touch of cynicism. She also writes a Jeevani Charika. Her books have been shortlisted for awards such as the RoNA Romantic Comedy of the Year (in 2017), Love Stories Award (in 2015) and the Joan Hessayon Award (2012).

Rhoda started off as a microbiologist and then drifted out of research and into technology transfer. When choosing a penname, she was hit by a fit of nostalgia and named herself after the bacterium she studied during her PhD.

She has lived in a variety of places including Sri Lanka, Yap (it's a real place), Halifax, Oxford and Didcot (also a real place). She now lives with her young family in East Yorkshire, where there are enough tea shops to keep her happy.

You can find her wittering on about cake and science and other random things on her website (http://www.rhodabaxter.com), on Facebook[1], or on Twitter (@rhodabaxter). Please do say hello if you're passing.

You can also follow her on Bookbub[2].

Don't forget, you can get a free copy of one of her books by joining her reader newsletter[3].

---

1. https://en-gb.facebook.com/RhodaBaxterAuthor/
2. https://www.bookbub.com/authors/rhoda-baxter
3. https://www.subscribepage.com/CforC

Copyright © Rhoda Baxter 2017

All rights reserved.

This is a work of fiction. Similarities to real people, places, or events are entirely coincidental.

www.rhodabaxter.com

Lightning Source UK Ltd.
Milton Keynes UK
UKHW011027271021
392923UK00004B/397